MAE MAE'S EASTEND CAFÉ

By

A Jean Jackson

A Sequel to: BLACKEYED PEAS AND CORNBREAD

DEDICATION: This book is dedicated to the generations of strong Black women in and close to my family. The women, my great grandmother Aggie Moore, my grandmother Sallie Moore Bates, other mentors and especially my mother Aggie Lucas Jackson, gave unselfishly to me, so that I could have a better life than they did. Thanks to the current family matriarch, my sister Francene McCray-Brown.

ACKNOWLEDGEMENTS: I express my sincere thanks to my dear lifetime friends, for all of their help and assistance with this book. Thanks to Ellen Taylor Atkins for her super radar proofreading. She read period to period and coma to coma with great precision. She is my sister from another mother. Thanks to Ann P. Graves for the cover photograph and to Beulah Renee Wells for the cover design. Thanks to Ellen Drehmann for my photo. And thanks to my family and extra special friends, who always support me in my quest to be a better author.

AUTHOR NOTES AND DISCLAIMER: This is a work of fiction. Names, characters, places and incidents are from the author's imagination and should not be construed as real. Though the names of churches, streets and communities in Asheville such as Eastend, Southside, Shiloh, and Stumptown mentioned in this book, actually exist, this book and all of the characters described are purely fiction. The use of the racial terms such as 'Colored,' 'Negro,' and White are not meant to be disrespectful, but are used in context based on the era portrayed in the book.

-Foreword-

Mae Mae's

Eastend Café is a continuation of the life and times of Mae Mae and her family and the role she played in the Eastend community, viewed from the inside of her Cafe. It is also about Mae Mae's daughter Esther, and her attempts to balance love, heartbreak and stardom. The family continues to search for the true meaning of love and 'family,' in hopes of improving with each generation.

The variety of characters who are Café patrons, show their need for a good time after working hard for 'the man,' then letting their hair down in the closeness of their own community.

In *Mae Mae's Eastend Café,* they dance, they sing, they gossip and they eat the best food in town. And whatever they do, they always come back for more, to the place that's just like home.

There is almost a constant pull of good and evil. Church plays a vital role in their lives. But they are also called to play the numbers, drink whiskey, and slow dance with somebody else's man (or woman).

Esther's sexy performances are the Saturday night draw for *Mae Mae's Eastend Café.* Her sultry voice and New York stardom, bring a special type of entertainment to Eastend. She connects with the community in a special way as Mae Mae looks on with pride. The kind of love she sings about is from the heart and real, yet will almost always be out of her reach.

The reader takes a visit to areas in the beautiful city of Asheville. The streets, the parks, the areas are very familiar to natives. Some areas existed and are now but a tinge of history, brought back to life. The beauty of the mountains and of nearby Cherokee, form a natural setting for the story.

As a native of Asheville, the story is from the author's heart. It serves as a history lesson packed with special times and special characters. This book is a sequel to her book, *BLACKEYED PEAS AND CORNBREAD.*

CHAPTER ONE

As enormous as the St. Lawrence Catholic Church is, it was packed with family, friends and curious onlookers. Located in Asheville, North Carolina, the Cathedral was like a decorative center piece for an otherwise dull and traditional downtown. But the centralized location made it easy to find. This was both a blessing and a curse for Mae Mae as she buried her child.

Of course, all of Mae Mae's faithful customers from her Eastend Café had come to show her their respect and support. That was a tradition in the close knit Eastend community. They put aside playing the 'numbas', the late night grinding slow dancing, and shots of whiskey, to support their respected old friend.

Attending a funeral of even a distant acquaintance was sort of expected. But this funeral was even more complicated than Mae Mae and her family could have imagined. There was no way Eastend could miss this one.

The Catholic funeral Mass was more quiet and ceremonious than Mae Mae was accustomed. She held back her expected family funeral shouts and moans though she wanted to reach deep down into her soul. Shouts were right on the fringes and right in her throat, but seemed so out of place here.

The White priest in his flowing white robes and his calm and quiet manner, seemed to be saying the usual banal Sunday Mass. But he was actually burying her child. For her and the other Eastend folks, much more drama was necessary and needed, whether it was real or not. When they buried a family member, God and everybody else had to hear their shouts.

In a moment of distraction, Mae Mae thought to herself how beautiful the church actually was. It was especially beautiful with the abundance of flowers covering the entire altar. She had never seen so many flowers in her life. And this abundance was always a show of respect in the community. Though the flowers would soon wilt and die, the goal was always to have as many as possible. The measurement of love and caring for the deceased showed in the numbers of flowers. And this kind of display certainly made Mae Mae proud.

Though calm and quiet, the high ceilings and the gigantic cross right in the center of the golden organ pipes at the front of the church, made the service seem fit for royalty. The casket was simply beautiful. Though it was wood, it was the most magnificent mahogany that money could buy. Mae Mae skipped no corners. "Only the best for my child," she said. "Nothin' but the best," she repeated, as she closed her eyes and drifted away.

"Mitch, you have to pick up Jacob this evening 'cause I'm in the studio," Esther said, with irritation in her voice. Mitch usually pitched in and did his part, but it seemed whatever he did was never enough for Esther.

"Ok! Ok!" he batted back. "I have things to do too. What time do I need to be there?"

"See that's what I'm talkin' about," she said. "You know as well as I do that we have to pick her up by 5:00."

They left it at that. Neither one of them enjoyed fighting even though that seemed to be all they did. It always worked out for the better because Esther was sickened by her own dominance and Mitch's deep love for her always silenced him before it was too late.

Arguments had become the norm since they moved to the suburbs of Washington DC with their baby, Little Jacob. They were always determined to show each other that the other person was wrong. Mitch wanted desperately to show that their love would grow with time. But Esther knew after the first year of marriage, that really loving him would never come to pass. They both knew they married for the wrong reasons. But at the time they said, "I Do," good sex seemed to be enough.

By 1958, the suburbs of DC were the perfect place for a successful Negro couple to have a good life. As a result of Esther's talent and Mitch's mind for business, they had done well. They wanted for nothing.

One thing was true, they had come a long way since leaving Eastend. The brick house with three bedrooms, two baths, an enormous kitchen, a dining room for entertaining and a fenced in back yard, was proof of just how far they had come.

Esther had no idea why she couldn't love Mitch. He was tall, high yellow and handsome with hair that he combed straight back highlighting sideburns and a neat mustache. He always dressed like a million dollars and would never be caught dead in anything less than a suit and tie with matching shoes.

These natural attributes and his way of always sporting the latest model Caddy, could turn the head of any woman. Yet since the day he heard the sound of her beautiful voice singing in *Mae Mae's Eastend Café* in 1941, Mitch longed only for Esther.

Now as an older adult, Esther, the thirty something singing sensation and mother was simply gorgeous. She had copper, lightly tanned skin, beautiful dark shoulder length hair, a perfect waistline and legs to die for. Those qualities and that beautiful smile made Esther simply unforgettable.

Fame seemed to come fast and easy for Esther. Playing the clubs in New York, a record deal and an album, followed by a few tours happened like it was meant to be. Rock and Roll and Gospel came naturally. And since those days of singing at St. James AME Zion church in Eastend, she knew without a doubt she could win over souls with her voice. Even if she had a lot of questions about God, she sang like a real child of God.

Her heart and soul were revealed in her voice, yet only through her singing. Once the show was over, her beauty remained, but the stage person disappeared.

The only person in the world that received her pure unadulterated love was Jacob. If anyone else including Mitch attempted to touch her, or hug her, she rejected them immediately. He knew his time to touch her was only in bed. On the right night and at the right time, the heat of their love making was so intense that neither of them knew where it came from. As a matter of survival, Mitch knew those times very well and he went for it.

"Where in the world have you been?" she asked, sitting in the dark, with more irritation in her voice than usual. "There is simply no excuse for this!"

"What? What you talking about?" he said, walking in turning on the lamp near her, then walking towards the well-stocked bar.

Esther looked so beautiful in the dim light that Mitch wished this was not a night when he had obviously messed up. Her skin tones were highlighted perfectly and the penetrating dark brown eyes looked like she could actually be an angel.

"Mitch! You know you said you would pick up Jacob! And here I am getting a call at 5:15 saying no one was there. What in heaven's name could make a man forget to pick up his own child? What could you possibly be doing that would make you forget him, Mitch?"

"Oh, Damn!" he said, knowing this would be a fight of fights. "I forgot, E. I totally forgot. I got to working on some stuff and then the fellows asked me to go out. I'm coming from *THE OMEGA.*"

"I should have known! Anytime you get with the fellows going to *THE OMEGA*, I can forget about getting any help around here. That's really messed up Mitch. Your baby boy who you claim to love, was sitting there waiting like he was an orphan. He had tears in his eyes like he really didn't trust that anybody was ever going to pick him up."

"Oh my goodness, Honey. I'm so sorry. You know Jacob's my heart. You know I would never do anything to hurt him."

"Well, you need to start proving that to me 'cause I'm just not convinced."

Mitch placed ice cubes in his gin and tonic without even thinking about it. The first sip was a big one. He knew two things. Their communication for the next few weeks would be colder than usual and he could forget about sex for a long, long time.

Esther was right. *THE OMEGA* was Mitch's downfall. It had become a safe haven for him since Litle Jacob's birth and their move to DC. Esther's coldness seemed to increase with time.

It was almost like her own baby, her own little person to love, was all she needed. And the colder she became the more familiar Mitch became with the club and doing his own thing. In the darkness of *THE OMEGA,* his best friends became gin and tonic.

He finished his drink and sat among the plush white cushions of the large couch where he knew he would end up tonight, drunk and sleep. This scene was happening more and more in his life. But he knew he would have to do better. He would have to do much better to keep his prize.

The ultimate approval came when he made it possible for Esther to perform. She needed to perform as much as Mitch needed to be intoxicated. It was how both of them got their fixes. For her it was a break from reality and facing all of the things that were missing in her life. It was a time when she could play dress up in fine clothes and seduce the audience with her eyes, her smile, her moves, her voice.

This night, her performance had been like all others. As she was ending the set, she said, "How many of you can feel me? Cause that's what it's all about...Feelin'. They call it soul ya'll," she said, laughing and taking a long drag from her cigarette.

She closed her eyes and as if making love to the mike, brought it within inches of her mouth. The slow rhythmic song she sang became a story she told. It was about life, about love, about broken hearts. It was about what each individual needed it to be, to do, and to feel. You could see it in their faces, in their tears. It was a magic emotion that Esther loved to stir in all who listened. It was her way, her moment to take control.

When the song was over she paused allowing everyone to go deeply into themselves before they were forced to return. Then she said in her sexiest voice, "Good night my 'Loves.'"

The set ended, but now her real work began. Now that most of her bookings were in the small intimate coffee house settings, she visited each table and pretended she liked the hugs, the smiles, the closeness. She had to be quick as she knew that soon the Cinderella feeling would disappear. She knew she had to get this done before she lost her silver slipper and had to run away.

Mitch walked over and saved her just in time. Right after a performance, he knew he was allowed to be closer. And knowing that time was ticking, he placed his arm around her waist, kissed her on the lips and excused her from the crowd as he whispered in her ear.

"Good job, E," he said, knowing how much she hated his forced kisses. He hoped things had cooled down by now, a couple of weeks since his failure to pick up Little Jacob. He prayed that her usual need for sexual intimacy after performing would kick in this time, no matter how angry she had been.

They retreated to the small lounge in the back. It was used more as a coat closet with a chair and a love seat. But it was just the space she needed to be away from the crowd as she came down from her natural high.

Esther inhaled long and deep. Mitch knew her usual pattern of behavior after the escape. So he stood back for a brief moment before going in for the test.

Her performances always played to him in a very special way. Raw sexiness and her unique ability to allow people deep inside of her soul hit Mitch twice as hard as everyone else. When everything was said and done, he was determined to have her.

Mitch wrapped his long arms around her, basically taking his chances and feeling out her mood. "Bingo," he thought to himself, when she didn't stiffen and pull away.

She received his tongue deep into her mouth holding on to the magic still hovering around them from her performance. These times were so intoxicating for him. With an otherwise cold human being reacting by reciprocating his touch, it became a maddening turn on for Mitch. At this level of intensity, they had to take it home.

The trip home was like it was in another realm. Yet reaching there had to have happened because the next thing they remembered, was being in the safe warmness of the silk sheets and large pillows in their gigantic oak, king sized bed.

The heat of their breathing was all about them as they kissed with the urgency of youngsters having sex for the first time. When she finally allowed him, Mitch knew exactly what he needed to do to please her. He devoured her, kissing her lips and her neck then lowering his head to each of her breasts.

He knew her weakness and used it to his advantage, taking his time to caress each one. She moaned as much from being sexually overpowered, as from being forced to do things her mind tried to reject.

After moments of necessary rediscovery, wetness signaled her readiness for him to enter her. For her these times, these moments served to inject her with staying power for him, for their marriage. He was hard to love but easy to take in as his manhood found her waiting mound. The time was short for them both, as they held on tight with simultaneous moans brought by extremely different reasons.

This was the pattern for them. Extreme heights of sexual aggression, that for her had more to do with need than love. For him it was simply collecting on the private debt she owed him because of marriage. This was life as they knew it.

CHAPTER TWO

Out of all of the funeral attendees, Marjorie was probably one of the only people who knew what was happening in the Catholic funeral mass. She followed right along standing and sitting on cue as well as responding to the priest in Latin. She proudly emphasized her familiarity with the rituals, speaking loudly and going through the motions like a pro.

A tall, gorgeous, middle aged women, Marjorie was a loyal Mae Mae supporter, who loved dancing into the late hours at the Café. Though married at least twice already, now she limited herself to slow dancing all night and then going home after a good time.

Perhaps that is why Mae Mae was so loved in the community. She literally wanted everyone who entered her Café's double doors, no matter what the circumstances, to have a great time.

Marjorie was Catholic though. She grew up near the 'mission church' across town called St. Anthony's of Padua. Mission church meant, being there for Colored converts who actually needed Catholicism to have salvation.

The church and the connecting school were headed by White priests and nuns who became like religious royalty to the families they served. They were authority figures who seemed to drop in, teach and spread the Word.

They came into the neighborhood just like missionaries in a foreign land. But the converts developed strong beliefs and passed those on to future generations.

Even for Marjorie though, St. Lawrence was somewhat foreign. Catholics from across the tracks like her, had only recently been able to attend the larger, better St. Lawrence Cathedral. The benefits of integration were fairly new. And the differences in the two churches were like night and day.

"May I speak to you in the kitchen for a moment, Mitch," Esther said, moving that way before he had the opportunity to reply.

She took a deep breath and tried to control her tone. But when Esther was angry or upset, this was hard to do. "I will not tell you again, Mitch! I won't tolerate your cussing in this house and especially around Jacob. Do you understand?"

Mitch didn't answer. He knew it would do no good. He simply looked down and let her continue.

"You know I cannot stand profanity. It turns my stomach like you would not believe. I grew up with my Mama cussing every other word and I will not let my Baby grow up like that. I just hate it, Mitch," she shouted. "I just hate it."

"OK! OK! I get it! I will try to restrain myself." He retreated without putting up any resemblance of a fight. They had had this conversation before. But in order to get his point across, sometimes profanity was the only language that flowed just right. "But she's right," he said to himself. "Mae Mae could cuss like a sailor."

They finished talking then reentered the large living room and found Little Jacob still playing with his plastic army men on the floor. He had a vivid imagination and could entertain himself for hours without a problem. And even with a collection of very expensive toys, he simply adored the cheaply made plastic toys that were a Christmas gift from Grandma Mae Mae. They never could see what he saw in the pale cheap little plastic toys. But since he always remained a quiet and content three year old, they simply went with the program.

"You ok, Jacob?" Esther asked, as she spotted him near the couch and paying them no attention.

"Yes!" he said, not even looking up from playing.

He was the spitting image of a combination of his mother and grandmother. He was going to be tall like Mae Mae with Esther's copper toned skin, and have the natural good looks of them both.

But his mother's Indian straight dark hair was missing. Instead, a mixture of both women left him with dark, long, wavy, thick hair. And for now, Esther was determined not to cut it.

"Daddy and I were trying to figure out if you want a big birthday party," Esther said, with manufactured excitement. "But you don't really like parties do you?" She added, teasing and trying to get a real response.

"Yes! Yes! Mommy," Jacob shouted, jumping up as his toys fell to the floor. "I love parties. Kin my friens' from play school come? Kin dey, Mommy?"

Mitch chimed in wanting to show that he played a part in these plans too. "You can invite whoever you want to, Big Boy. You're getting to be so big. You're gonna be four years old right?"

Esther thought to herself. "Time really does fly. It seems like yesterday when I went back to Asheville from New York, pregnant, unhappily married, and searching for the truth about my own family. That was 1955, and I've come a long way since then."

She looked over at Mitch as he picked up their son and swung him around in a circle. "We could be such a wonderful family if only I could love Mitch like I should," she thought, seeing so clearly how much he loved Jacob. "Now my Baby is about to have his fourth birthday. Yep, time really passes fast."

Mitch put Jacob down followed by a kiss on his cheek. "I'm going out for a bit," he said to Jacob, though really meant it for Esther. "I'm gonna bring you back a big surprise."

"And where are you going?" Esther asked, trying hard to keep the tension out of her voice,

"I've got a late meeting," he said, knowing it was not enough information for her, but it was as much as he would offer. "I won't be too late."

"Well this is getting to be a habit," she said sarcastically. "I know all of the performance dates are set for the next three months. Unless you know something that I don't." She got closer and whispered, "why don't you just go on and tell the truth? If you got another woman out there somewhere, just say so."

"E, you know I love you dearly," he said honestly, but returning her sarcasm. "Seeing another woman is the last thing I would leave this house to do. I can't wait for you to see the things I'm setting up for you. I'm hookin' you up with some mighty big people in this business."

"Well, only God knows what you're up to out there in those streets," she said. "I've never seen anyone go out night after night on business and stay out 'til all hours of the night. But you go right ahead. At least you get me the gigs. I've never had any complaints about that. We've never had a problem getting me on stage and payin' the bills."

Mitch slipped away and up the stairs to the bedroom. He found just the right suit and matching shoes. He dressed, tipped down the stairs, slipped out the door to the garage and quietly backed out in his 1959 Cadillac.

This bar was dark and shabby. It was not at all like *THE OMEGA*. This one was on the side of DC that Esther would never be caught dead in. She likely had no idea this other side of the tracks existed. It was a world which Mitch had come to know well and it had become another one of his secrets.

"What you got tonight, Man?" he said, talking to Greg, a heavy, light-skinned, short dude with processed hair.

"I got whatever you need, Man," Greg said boasting. "I been tryin' to git you off that sissy reefer ta try some of this other real stuff I got. I told you 'bout it last time."

"Well I gotta long way to go home, so I can't be all messed up like that," Mitch said. "I just want a nice mellow high. Just give me a nickel bag, Man. You don't know my Old Lady. I have to be cool by the time I get back to the house," he said with a chuckle.

"Well you come to the right place," Greg said, reaching into his bag and coming out with the goods. "That'll be twenty bucks."

Mitch pulled out his wallet and handed Greg two twenties. One twenty was for the nickel bag. The other was to express true thanks for the substance he yearned for as much as he yearned for Esther. It was like he had found a way to fill in the missing gaps in his relationship with her. Weed helped him make sense of it all, even if only for a moment.

The *GAP BAR* existed mainly for the purpose of drug distribution. With its dark ragged appearance and questionable patrons, there was no other reason on earth anyone would want to be at this bar.

What could be seen of the wood floor was dirty. The bar stools had seen better days a long time ago. The rips and tears showed more dirty cotton stuffing than the plastic covering. The only lighting was the shiny old beer ads hanging over the bar. The lighting showed a brief look into the sad wanting eyes around the entire room.

Mitch slid away into the men's room. How even a moment's peace and escape could be experienced in the midst of the smell and filth of this room was unimaginable. Yet time after time, Mitch and the other lost souls accomplished just that. He took his time, rolling the joint perfectly then lighting up. It had been a while since he visited *THE GAP,* so he took in his first drag slowly and deeply. He closed his eyes after the third draw, waiting for the high to kick in.

"This is good shit," he said to himself, not realizing he was saying it out loud. "I need to cut this out," he said laughing. "If 'E' find out, she'll kill me."

The drive home was smooth as he listened to Sam Cook on the radio and cruised along. It was later than usual, so he prepared himself mentally for the impending altercation. "What a way to mess up a good high," he said to himself and smiled.

CHAPTER THREE

It was hard to believe that the organist at the Funeral Mass was actually a Negro woman. When several attendees glanced behind them and up into the choir loft way up high and behind them, there was no doubt. Why then, they thought, wasn't she rockin' that organ? Why was the music so plain and dull and White?

Ms. Lealah was not just the organist. She was the Catholic Liturgy organist. In fact, she had been a part of the natural integration process of moving the entire congregation from St. Anthony's Catholic Church, located in Southside, to the St. Lawrence Cathedral, located in downtown Asheville. Mrs. Hutcher simply came with the package, like trading pitchers in pro league baseball.

So, the slow non-rhythmic music the Eastend folks heard at the Funeral Mass was within the boundaries of Catholicism, just like the Mass itself. This would have been true regardless of who and what race actually played the organ.

Ms. Lealah could be described as just music. While playing she exhibited no personality and no character. Her goal was just to accompany Catholics as they arrived, during and as they departed Mass.

But she was actually more than just music. She was educated at Spelman College in Atlanta. She married Dr. Neeman Hutcher, one of a few Negro dentists in Asheville. And she lived in a beautiful ranch style home in the Negro suburbs, called Shiloh.

It was a time when dental work for most Negroes in Asheville and elsewhere amounted to simply getting teeth pulled. There was no such thing as preventative dentistry. Most were so poor that they went to the dentist when their teeth hurt so badly that they absolutely had to go. But still the Hutcher's were considered upper-crust Negroes, and they lived well.

Today she played for the Funeral Mass. She played for Mae Mae, the grieving mother, even though she'd never met her before in her life. What Mae Mae and the other Eastend crowd didn't know was that Ms Lealah played the same old tunes that were usual and predictable for any Catholic Funeral Mass. But because it was them, people who "looked like her," she played even better.

Balloons and kids were everywhere. Esther was happy that the predicted rain had passed over because the party could now be in the large back yard as planned. So on April 11 in the spring of 1959, Jacob was as happy as ever entertaining his friends.

The clown and the magician were a big hit and had already done their thing. So the kids just played hide and seek and tag. They all played like their energy could go on forever. They ate and had their fill of ice cream, cake, candy and popcorn. This was a party like none other. It was what they could afford and what Esther and Mitch desired to give their only child.

After a while you could see the children winding down in the early evening. It had been a long day with lots of activity. And by now parents were anxious to leave to take advantage of the tiredness now evident in their kids. So his friends said their goodbyes as Little Jacob stood by sadly and waved.

"Well, you have a good time?" Mitch asked.

"Yes Daddy! I had fun with my friends," he said, jumping up and down. "I always wanted a party just like that."

"Well you need to be sure to thank Mommy," he said, with love pouring from his voice.

"We wanted you and your friends to have a great time."

"That's right Baby!" Esther chimed in. "Mommy and Daddy love you so much," she said, giving Jacob a big hug.

"But guess what? It's time for you to go night, night," Esther said. "Head on up and I'll be right behind you to tuck you in."

After the amazing party, you could see the tiredness in his eyes as Jacob kissed them and said goodnight. He climbed the stairs leading to his room and waved at the top. The house was finally quiet.

Mitch was feeling the itch. But he had no idea how to tell Esther after such a peaceful day. He knew he would have to tell her a lie to get out and get what he needed. This was necessary, but was never easy.

"E," he said, getting a feel for her mood more than anything else. "I did the Daddy thing all day and I just need to get away for a minute. You OK with that?"

She took the deep breath that always seemed necessary for her to deal with Mitch. Her mood changed much too quickly. It changed from the joy of the big celebration of Little Jacob's fourth birthday, to the hell she endured with a husband she never wanted. She had never had a close relationship with God, but she needed something, someone now to make things better.

"I knew it was coming, Mitch," she said. "I can tell when you get antsy and need to get away. Just go! Don't make apologies, don't ask permission, and don't even feel bad. Just go!"

He said nothing more and simply turned to climb the stairs. The suit he usually wore to *THE GAP* was at the back of the closet. This was partly to keep it 'out of sight out of mind' and partly to hide the powerful smell that could reveal his secret.

He dressed as if going to a luxury destination, but knowing privately it would be another trip into the filth of *THE GAP*. Regardless of the terrible awaiting conditions, the outcome would be the same. If only momentary, for him it would be pure unadulterated joy.

He found Greg in his usual place at the bar. Again this time Greg offered a different and better high. But this time Mitch did not refuse. "You got coke?" he asked. "I need something hard tonight."

After they settled, Mitch took his usual place in the second stall of *THE GAP* men's room. After a long day of child's play and replacing his usual couple of joints with the powerful white powder, it

25

didn't take long for him to reach the ultimate high. He enjoyed it too much. And what felt like moments turned to hours of nodding and a deep sleep. Then suddenly he awakened to a loud knock on the door of the stall.

"If anyone is in there, come out!" the voice shouted. "You and everyone else in here, is under arrest for the possession of drugs."

Mitch swallowed hard. He was more frightened of what Esther would say and do than the possibility of going to jail. He thought the dealers at *THE GAP* maintained a good relationship with the cops. But this night something had fallen through the cracks. Something had gone terribly wrong. It was something way beyond Mitch's control.

Handcuffs were placed on Mitch, Greg, all of the dealers and three other men as they were taken away. The men were placed in four separate patrol cars which meant the cops knew the number of perpetrators before their arrival. How they knew, nobody could figure it out.

At the station, Greg and the other men seemed almost familiar with the arrest procedures. Mitch however was a nervous wreck as they patted them down, took their mug shots and pushed them into a room to change clothes.

His tailored suit and matching shoes were out of place among the others. But as he thought about this minor detail, a gray prison suit and plastic slide on shoes were thrown in his direction.

The attire brought a sudden reality to Mitch. None of this was not a dream. What started as his occasional need for drugs and alcohol began to demand more and more of him. He had lost control and the desire began to take over. It was a great night for law enforcement and a bad night for the rest of the world. Life for Mitch, Esther and Little Jacob would never be the same again.

CHAPTER FOUR

*As the funeral progressed, the choir sang
along with the enormous pipe organ delivering a
sound and a song that Mae Mae did not understand.
They repeated Latin phrases in response to the
priest and it was a language she and the others did
not know.*

*It was beautiful and very different, but it just
didn't get down into her soul like her church always
did. This sound lacked the loud, rhythmic, powerful
Gospel beat that she always heard at St. James
AME Zion Church, literally in the center of
Eastend.*

*St. Lawrence Cathedral was so drastically
different that Mae Mae almost doubted if God could
really hear them. She wondered if this lack of loud
energetic praise would be enough to get her baby
even close to the 'Pearly Gates.'*

*Not just Mae Mae, but everyone from the
Eastend crowd looked lost and puzzled about the
flow of the service. Each and every one of them
thought something was missing. It was like they
were in a foreign land simply observing and going
through the motions.*

*The casket at the front of the church was the
only thing familiar to most of them. But the
beautiful silk cloth covering it with the large, red
cross in the middle, even made that different.*

*Mae Mae took pause and looked at each of
the figures exhibiting the Stations of the Cross. They
hung around the perimeter inside of the church as a
reminder of Jesus' pain and suffering as he traveled*

to his death on the cross. And though crosses were everywhere as a reminder of Christ's sacrifices for us, it was hard for Mae Mae to find him here.

As she looked around at those present at this special home going, she could not help but think about how they all got here. So much had happened that brought them all to this place and time.

The *Mae Mae's Eastend Ca*fé was Mae Mae's jewel. To be Negro and female and actually own a business was for the most part unheard of in Asheville in the 1960's. Actually her life and fortune had changed long before and in the 40's with the death of her beloved Ma Letty.

After being literally dropped on Ma Letty's doorstop as an eighteen year old, her life would never be the same. It was a blessing that changed her life, and that she would never forget.

Ma Letty worked hard and she worked for herself. She not only passed on that work ethic to Mae Mae, but she also left her the insurance money that would help her to own her dream Café. The insurance policies bought the building at the corner of Mountain and Pine Streets right in the center of the Eastend community.

One large room with a bar and eight booths greeted customers at the entrance. A clean wood floor bordered black and white diamond linoleum squares in the center. Silver stands holding bar stools with padded red seats, lined the bar awaiting familiar regulars.

Beer ads were behind the bar and the back room that was added in the 50's with intimate seating and a stage, was just large enough for jukebox slow dancing or special performances.

The Café was especially crowded tonight. The small stage in the corner of the room was perfect now that Esther had returned. At least once a month she was scheduled to perform for the intimate crowd that gathered there. Getting a seat was difficult to impossible.

Mae Mae just loved having Esther and Little Jacob back in Asheville. Esther's performances were just icing on the cake. And the Eastend crowd could not get enough of her. Their own Esther, the star, was back at home, just for them.

"How's everyone tonight?" Esther asked into the mic. She was really sincere and seriously asking each and every individual present in the room. "It's Friday night ya'll," she laughed sending her head way back. "Ya'll been slavin' all week long. Now come on and get down with me on this Friday night."

They all clapped returning the energy, feeding her just the way she loved. She had a way of talking to each person and having her own intimate time with each one. She knew how to work a room, whether it was the small stage at *Mae Mae's Eastend Café* or a big concert hall in New York City.

She started to sing 'Strange Kind o' Love,' as the crowd smiled and clapped with instant familiarity. It was her first hit song and they remembered the words better than she did. *"Every love just ain't the same. Some is good and some is strange,"* she sang almost effortlessly. *"Some I give and some I make. Some ain't worth the time it take. It's strange. Strange Kind o' Love."*

The crowd didn't want it to end. They never did. In these days and times, this was their escape. Being in *Mae Mae's Eastend Café*, grooving to the voice of Esther, momentarily took them away from the cruel world that was most everywhere else.

Many of those in the Eastend crowd worked for 'the Man' all week long. They worked damn hard. They put up with inferiority in most aspects of life, everywhere they went. But not here. Not now.

Esther lit a cigarette and inhaled deeply, holding the smoke as it became a part of her. She knew the crowd needed her. She knew why they were there. And she took her time and gave them just that. But after four soul-filled songs she had to let it go. It was all she had to give.

The ice in her glass of bourbon had long since melted after her second song. Refusing to let it go, she still turned it up and drained it. As she lowered her glass, Mae Mae approached with a big smile.

"Oh Baby!" Mae Mae exclaimed. "You always do so good out there."

"Thanks," Esther said, with a lot less enthusiasm. "I'm just here, 'cause I just couldn't take DC any longer after Mitch got put away."

"I know, Baby. That's jus' awful. I'm so sorry about dat, but I'm glad as hell you here."

"Mama, don't start that cussin'," Esther said. "You know how much I hate that!"

Mae Mae hadn't changed much at all in the years since Esther escaped Asheville with Mitch. She had aged slightly and had a few grey hairs, but she was an attractive fifty-five year old. Her beautiful dark skin was still without flaws and her tall thin frame showed no signs of old age weight gain. Basically she was a tall, dark, attractive yet seasoned woman.

"You hungry?" Mae Mae asked Esther, changing the subject. "I know you haven't eat nothin' all evenin' long. Big Jimmie fixed some pork chops, collards and mashed potatoes tonight dats out o' dis worl'."

"That sounds good Mama," Esther chimed in, cutting her off. "I'm gonna call home and check on Jacob, then I'll be in the booth in the back."

By now, most of the regulars knew not to approach her as she walked about after her performance. They knew that where they truly got a piece of Esther was when she was on stage. She momentarily freed them with her soothing voice and then they allowed her freedom and privacy afterwards.

She slid into the booth. There was always just enough light in that back booth to see and hear only what was desired. It had become her perfect get away at the perfect time. This was where Esther went back inside of herself. This was where she took back all that she so graciously gave away in her performance.

"Hello stranger," a voice called out to her after she settled comfortably into her booth. Her eyes were closed and her head was leaning back.

"Hearing your beautiful voice, brought back such memories for me that I couldn't resist coming over to say hello. I hope you don't mind."

She looked up slightly irritated and puzzled, but soon after, a big smile appeared. It was like a fairy tale. It was a face from long ago, yet one she would never forget. It was one she had dreamed of many times. It was Frank Jordan, her first true love.

"Frank?" she said, with a question in her tone, yet knowing without a doubt who it was. "Is that you? You haven't changed a bit."

He smiled that smile she remembered so well. It highlighted beautiful brown skin, straight white teeth, a thick mustache and neatly cut hair.

Frank Jordan was always handsome as a young teenager in high school. But as an adult, a man, he was beyond good looking. Esther noticed this immediately and it made her smile.

"Please sit down and join me," she said. "I'm getting ready to eat a bite. Can we get you anything?"

"No. No thanks, "he said. "I can't stay long. I'd heard what a sensation you were here in Eastend so I just couldn't resist any longer. I just had to come out and see for myself."

"Well we have to get together again and catch up real soon then," she said disappointed. "It seems like ages since I saw you last."

"Sounds good," he said. "I promise I will be in touch soon. He left an imprint of that famous smile, as he turned and departed.

Esther's thoughts were dancing all over the place. As hungry as she had been before he spoke to her, she did not touch her food. The meat loaf, mashed potatoes with gravy, collard greens and cornbread served only as props for the very new chapter in her life.

"Was that who I thought it was?" Mae Mae asked, as she approached the booth. "I haven't seen that boy, Frank Jordan, but a few times since you left for New York. They say he live in a nice house out in Shiloh with a wife and a baby boy."

"Oh! So he's married huh?" Esther asked, with a tone like she didn't really care.

"Yep! Been running numbas up on Eagle Street foreva'. Married dat lady name o' Mildred dat do hair in that shop near the cab stand. "

"Oh, I remember her from Stephens Lee. She was a really pretty girl in high school. I can see Frank getting hooked up with her."

"Yeah an' she ownin' that beauty an' barber shop. So they doin' pretty good. Some o' those houses out in Shiloh is real nice."

"But 'numbers runnin,' Mama?" Esther said, in disbelief, "Frank couldn't do any better than that?"

"Girl!" Mae Mae said shaking her head, with a slowly emerging smile. "Some o' the richest Negroes in Asheville runnin' numbas. Seem like since it don't hurt nobody and they can have nice cars and nice homes, that's what some o' 'em do.

"Most of 'em don't even mix that Eagle Street stuff wit' dey home life. They still live in good neighborhoods on the otha' side o' town, go to church every Sunday and live the good life."

"Well, I know at Stephens Lee High School, Frank Jordan was one of the smartest guys there. He was a real good student. I just thought he would have made more of his life."

"Everybody do the best dey can, Honey. Just like you did. And things turned out just fine for you, right?"

"I guess so, Mama. But I still have a long way to go."

CHAPTER FIVE

The priest looked out at the faces looking back at him in the large sanctuary. Truthfully, he seldom knew those people in the casket laying before him or the relatives and following they may have had. His goal was to put on the best show he could within the confines of the church traditions and his ability to connect (or not) in a very short time.

In some ways he hid behind the formality of the rituals of the Mass. There was only a brief time during the service when he had to break from the set script. And those times that were somewhat similar to 'preachin' were the times he hated most. The very personalized service of a funeral made it even harder.

He looked down and over the very formal altar at Mae Mae noting that she was the mourning mother. Looking away briefly he noticed how attractive she was for an older Negro woman. Though he attempted to never really see the beauty in any woman, he really hated the things going through his head, particularly about a woman of color.

This woman, this mother's true loss was very obvious to him. Deep in her eyes he could see her heartbreak and pain. He could see a sadness that revealed her heart and soul.

A life of great loss, pain and trouble jumped out at him. In fact, he noted, that most of the people attending this funeral had a similar look in their eyes. Those looks were about more than the current

expressions of grief and sympathy. Perhaps that
sadness was natural for the entire race of Negroes.
Whatever it was, it was powerful, and it could be
felt coming from everyone in the church.

He was self-conscious as he began to speak
and could sense whatever he was saying and
whatever words he chose, were just not enough.

The faces showed that they were looking for
more, they needed much more from him. They
wanted his words to move them and to bring them
closer to God. But no matter what he said, there
seemed to be no true connection.

Mae Mae had tried for months to persuade
Esther to attend church with her. But since Esther's
arrival back in Asheville, she had had no luck
winning that battle. During that time in Esther's life
when she sang in the church, she had been a faithful
young believer.

But after the trauma inflicted on her as an
innocent girl by her stepfather, 'Preacher,' faith in
God was hard for her. Esther could sing Gospel
straight from the depths of her heart and soul. But
true faith in God for her was a whole 'nother story.

At this time in Mae Mae's life, no doubt
about it, she truly needed God. And though she
played the Blues on Saturday nights in the Café
while the Eastend crowd slow dragged in the dark
corners, God was always close by her. Everyone
knew it and everyone knew that Gospel and only
Gospel played in her Café on Sundays after church.
That was an undebatable law.

"I'm headed to St. James this morning,"
Mae Mae said to Esther. "And I'm gonna take Jacob
wit' me. You sure you don't want to come?' she
said, knowing the answer already.

"Nope! Maybe one day, Mama." She said,
watching them go out the door.

Moments later, Mae Mae and Jacob entered
St. James and seated themselves on the left of the
sanctuary close to the center of the church. She
possessively claimed the same seat she had sat in
for years. It was a right-of-passage. The older a
member was, the more entitled they were to their
chosen seat. This was an unspoken right purchased
with age and longevity.

Jacob jerked around as the men's choir
entered from the back. Their jet black suits with
white dress shirts and black bow ties were sharp, as
no particular man stood out, but they all did.

They took their time taking one step at a
time in unison and in beat with the rocking organ
chords. Eyes were straight ahead as if they were on
a mission and nothing could stop them.

The front platform and choir seats awaited
them as their slow steps brought them closer and
closer. As a group, they made music before they
even sang the first note.

Reverend Goins was seated, waiting
patiently. He sat majestically like the person in
charge taking command before a word was spoken.

Dressed in a dark tailored suit covered with
a colorful vestment, his shiny black shoes crossed at
the ankle, and spoke of his manliness. Sharing his
knowledge of the Word was his reason for being

there. But his own persona almost over shadowed his true purpose, which was preaching God's Word.

Once the choir was in place at their seats it signaled to the Revered that he was 'on'. He stood and walked to the podium slowly, as if everyone present had no choice but to wait for his first words. On this day and at this time, he was the star.

"Good Morning, Church!" he said with a chuckle. *"This is the day the Lord has made. Let us rejoice and be glad.* Yes! Rejoice! Church!" he shouted. "It's OK to rejoice."

The congregation including Mae Mae reacted as if they knew something great was about to follow. Just the few words spoken by the Reverend created a high in the room. Everyone knew it would begin with a spark and grow into something none of them controlled. None of them cared to control it.

"Church! Do ya'll know what it means to have faith? What it really means?" he asked, knowing he would tell them anyway. "Open yo' Bible an' take a look at Hebrews 11:1. Let me quote just what it says 'cause can't nobody say it like the actual Word say it. Amen? Amen.

"It says, *'Now faith is confidence in what we hope for an' assurance about what we do not see.'* Now dats a few word dat say an' awful lot. Can I git an Amen, Ya'll?"

"Amen!" they shouted, assured that the more they participated the more he would perform for the primary purpose of teaching them the Word.

"Now for me, one of the best examples of faith appears in Matthew 9:20. Let us all turn to that scripture. *'And, behold a woman who was diseased with an issue of blood twelve years, came behind him and touched the hem of his garment.'*

"Well folks, I hate to tell you, but she knew it was against the law for her to even be around other people with a problem of that nature. But her faith was so strong, she believed that all she had to do was touch the hem of Jesus' garment, and she would be healed. Oh my God! Now that's faith, Church!

"Can you see it? Do you even sense that level of faith that she had? She didn't want to bother him by asking him for nothing. She didn't want to push in front of anyone else to get his attention. She just wanted to be healed. And out of all of the other folks pushin' and shovin', her faith was so strong even Jesus felt it and he had to ask, 'who touched Me?'

"Oh Lord Jesus! I don't think ya'll git it! Ya'll not feelin' me," he said, skipping across the platform, clapping his hands. "People! Just like that woman, you got to believe that what you need and what God wants for you, if you believe, it will be given to you.

"Faith! Faith! Faith! This ain't no game! Church! You not gonna be nothin' or have nothin' without first having faith."

They were really feeling him now and reacting accordingly. Shouts rang from the pews and echoed back circling like a hurricane. The energy he gave them they gave right back, as they

stood on their feet clapping, hungry for more.
Nothing could stop him now.

"The Bible is full of examples of faith,
Ya'll. Look at John second Chapter where it speaks
of turning water into wine. Do you even think
Mary, Jesus' mother, could have turned to her Son
in a panic and said, 'Son you got to do something
about this wine situation!' without faith?

"And Matthew 14:29, Church, is a big one.
*'And he said Come, and when Peter was come down
out of the ship, he walked on water to go to Jesus.'*
Need I say more?

"Yes, we call ourselves prayin' all the time.
And though we should pray and let it go, because of
what? Yes, Faith. We keep askin' and askin' and
askin', thinkin' God don't hear us. He hears us,
Ya'll. But our faith is what helps us to let go and let
God take over. God's love for us wants us to have
the best of everything.

"He has plans for each and every one of us.
Just take a quick look at Jeremiah 29:11. And I'm
gonna close, I promise. It says, *'For I know I have
plans for you saith the Lord, thoughts of peace, and
not of evil, to give you an expected end.'*

"He can do anything," he said, very quietly.
"Faith is all you need."

The congregation stayed on their feet the
entire time. It was as if they didn't want to miss the
blessings and wanted to hold on to every single
word. They were sweating and shouting and feeling
what God sent him to say. The Holy Spirit filled the
room and moved them to another realm.

As he sat down everyone could see that it was over. As quickly as it started and the necessary points were made, he retreated to give them time to digest it all. He wiped the sweat from his brow, then waved his hand like a magician and the choir to begin to sing.

Mae Mae gave Jacob a big hug hoping her loving touch would somehow transfer the wisdom and Godly lessons they both had heard. The Grandmother wanted to take it in, chew it and digest it for her grandchild.

With all of the ugliness and hurt that had occurred in their family, she knew God and only God could save the generations to come. It was her responsibility to pass on the goodness to correct their horrible past.

They departed the church holding hands. The joy in their hearts was there, but from different places and for different reasons. One was happy to hear the plain and simple Word of God in a way she could understand. The other was just happy to be in the midst of something so large, even if it was more than he could understood at such a young age.

CHAPTER SIX

Ms. Owens glanced to her right at the beautiful St. Lawrence stained glass windows. The reds, the blues, the greens were placed together so perfectly that the Blessed Virgin in her flowing robes and bright yellow halo, was simply magnificent.

She noticed that each window performed its own artful purpose. Each one showed a visual testimony to everyone who viewed them. All she knew was, regardless of how different it looked and how different it felt from her own St. James, it was simply beautiful.

The other stained glass window closer to the back really intrigued her. It pictured Jesus carrying a single sheep on his shoulders. And it reminded her of the story she had told to her Sunday school classes for many years.

Ms. Owens was known for always teaching the second graders at the St. James AME Zion Church and at the Mountain Street School. For her, the two went hand in hand. But this lovely creation that caught her eye, spoke loudly of the Bible verse she loved and taught to those children she called 'her Babies.'

She recalled that John 10:4-5 was a perfect verse for young ones to understand. It reads, **4-** *"And when he putteth forth his own sheep, he goeth before them and his sheep follow, for they know his voice. 5-And a stranger they will not follow, but will flee from him: for they know not the voice of strangers."*

The relationship of the sheep to the Master is so powerful in this chapter of John. And the stained glass window in St. Lawrence Catholic Church depicted it so well.

Her second graders would love to see this work of art, she thought. She knew they would be able to understand it so much better by actually seeing it pictured on the window. Learning by seeing was always her goal with her 'Babies'.

Sometimes it was tough, given the resources they had. But the constant challenge of using passed on books, filled with White kids doing White things actually made her a better teacher.

Ms. Owens was one of many Negro teachers at Mountain Street School whose goal was to provide the best education possible, regardless of the shortage of the resources they really needed. They used hand-me-down books and students sat in second-hand desks. And teachers, like Ms. Owens, didn't miss a beat.

But the schools were on the fringes of a mass integration. And teachers like Ms. Owens couldn't help but wonder if this 'fix' would really be better for their 'Babies.' They wondered if separate but 'supposedly' equal was actually the best solution.

They knew that the teachers who inherited their 'Babies' by way of forced integration, would never love or care about educating them like they did.

"Stop thinkin' about teaching," she thought to herself, as she looked up at the altar, hearing but not understanding anything the priest was saying.

"I'm not here this day as a teacher. I'm here for Mae Mae. Everyone from all walks of life love and respect Mae Mae because she's always there for the church and the community. Looks like everyone turned out for her today."

"Hello there! I said I'd be back," a familiar voice called out into the dimly lit room.

Esther looked up and to her surprise, her dream had finally come true. Months after their original encounter, Frank Jordan stood before her smiling that irresistible smile. She tried her best not to smile or to show her surprise. Though she had longed for him since the last time she saw him, she could never let him know.

"Well, if it isn't Frank Jordan," she said, with false disinterest in her voice. "What brings you back this evening?"

Frank smiled that irresistible smile showing beautiful white teeth and those unforgettable features. She tried not to stare and to glance up, avoiding the eyes. Looking into those eyes she knew would be her downfall. But what he could not see and what would not give her away was her rapid heartbeat.

"I've been busy lately," he said. "But I knew you would be performing tonight and there was no way I could miss it. Your name is big here in Asheville. That sound you have is unmistakable."

She hid her blush in the darkness wanting him to stay and talk, but refusing to let him know. Never the less, he sat down opposite her in the booth and said nothing. He just looked into her eyes as she resisted no longer and looked right back.

The heat between them exploded while rewinding them back to their young innocent days when they first met. The look in their eyes held on to the time between them as if it had never passed. She fought it with everything she had, while he welcomed the moment with no regrets. Then as suddenly as it began it ended and both of them looked away.

As if that magical but brief moment never happened, she said, "Well, why don't you relax for a while since we didn't get a chance to really catch up last time you were here. Come on! Catch me up on all those years since I left Asheville."

Frank smiled that smile again, knowing already how it automatically lit up her eyes. His immediate response showed that he had thought deeply about this reunion too. There was a lot to share and he knew it.

"Yea, I've got some time," he said. "But you've got some sharing to do too. I know you've been doing more than just breaking hearts with that voice of yours."

He breathed in deeply not knowing quite where to begin. "First of all, just know how much it broke my heart when you left town. I was what they call, 'young and in love' and thought you felt the same way."

Esther looked away blinking back tears that insisted on coming to her eyes. Her heart beat faster and faster as she listened to him speak. Broken hearts were not meant for the kind of love they shared then. Time that passed had apparently made it worse.

"But anyway," Frank continued, "I finished Stephens Lee High and worked some odd jobs here and there for a while, but never really wanted to leave town.

"Maybe it was my memories of you that kept me here. Or maybe I just didn't have that sense of adventure like you did," he said looking up dreamily. "Life goes on though and after a few years, I thought it was about time to settle down.

"I got married to another one of our Stephens Lee classmates, but not until a few years after you left town. You remember Mildred Allen don't you? She was short with long hair and real big shapely hips."

"Huh, yes. I knew her, but we never really hung out together. She was from Southside, right?

"Yep, she was after me like a dog in heat," he said, with a chuckle. "But for the longest time, I just did my school work and left all of the girls alone. After I graduated, I messed around some until I decided to finally settle down. Just turned out that Mildred was still waiting in the wings."

"I bet she was," Esther said, followed by a loud laugh.

"It was one of those things where I knew I'd never love her, but both of us always knew it. We made the best of our lives and to this day we are best friends. In fact when she heard you were back in town, she betted me that it would be a matter of time and I would have to see you."

"Well, I guess she got that part right. But please reassure her my dear, I am not back in Asheville to take nobody's man."

"So it's like that, huh?" he said teasing. "No I can't say I ever got over you. But both of us went on with our lives. And they say, 'You should never look back'."

Sadness reflected in the eyes of both of them. As if they were looking down into a wishing well seeing the beauty of something that was unattainable. It seemed that love alone was not enough to turn back the hands of time. But their dreams never really changed.

"I hear you have a little boy too. Right?" Esther asked, changing the subject.

"Yep!" Frank said with excitement. "I've got a terrible two year old. His name is Jack and he is my heart. Talking about love, now he is the love of my life."

"I'm so happy for you Frank. I have a 5 year old named Jacob and I love him the same way. He kept me going when I thought I couldn't make it some days."

"So, tell me about your work," Esther changed the subject again, anxious to know every detail. "I hear you lead an exciting life up there on Eagle Street. I hear you've done OK for yourself."

He laughed deeply, leaning his head way back. "And who in the world's been telling you all of those stories?" he asked, through his amusement.

"Oh, you know there are no secrets among us Negroes in Asheville," she said. "Everybody knows everybody's business."

"Well, I guess you could say, I do alright," Frank replied. "I just got tired of working for 'Da Man.' It was too much like slavin' every day and never having nothing to show for it.

"So this man named Mr. Mitchell took me under his wing and taught me everything he knew about running numbers. You know here they call it the 'Bo-Leeta.' It's popular, it's profitable, it's been around longer than dirt, and it's quietly illegal," he said with a chuckle.

"You know, the old heads, Mr. Mitchell, and Jack Crawford and all of them taught us that the key is keeping the cops happy. As long as they get paid, we're in business. And yes, a few of us have done very well," he said, flashing that smile that she loved to see. "OK! OK! Enough about me now. I've told you everything. Now it's your turn."

Esther smiled with a shyness that took over her face, knowing her time would come but not knowing where to start. Those horrible times of being assaulted by Preacha and Elijah flooded her brain. Those times had forced her to leave, regardless of her love for Frank. Those times were family secrets that Frank could never know.

"So now you know about Little Jacob, which means I stayed still long enough to have a child," she said with a nervous laugh. "I left Asheville because for my own sanity, I just needed to get away, OK. Just know that it had nothing to do with you. I was in love with you too, but there was a lot going on in my family, that's all.

"You remember Mitch that use to hang around my Mom's Café? Well, he was a lot older

49

than me and was always saying he could make me a star. So, after all that was going on with me, I finally took him up on it."

Frank was quiet but thoughtful. She could see the questions rolling around in his head. But he kept them to himself. At least for now.

"Mitch and I went away to New York. At first we were struggling like you wouldn't believe. He had a little money in the beginning, but of course that didn't last long. But he was good to me. He really was. If I can say anything about Mitch, he loved me and would do anything in the world for me.

"He had to do some questionable things to get money for a while. But he was super protective of me and would never let anyone touch me in the wrong way. Putting me out there sexually for money was out of the question with Mitch.

"Anyway he knew some people, who knew some people that were in the music business. And once Mitch got up with them and they heard me sing, then there was no turning back. Things were moving so fast and basically Mitch kept his promise. When I looked around, I was hearing myself on jukeboxes."

"Yep," Frank said. "I remember that. At first you sang under the name 'Queen.' But there was no mistaking that voice. The home folks in Asheville knew that was you."

"After all of that, Mitch thought it would make more sense for us to be married. So between shows we snuck off to the Justice of the Peace, and that was that."

"That simple, huh?" Frank asked.

"Yes, that simple," she repeated. "To tell the truth, it sounds very much like your relationship with Mildred. The only difference is you're still with her."

Both of them just laughed, as they just held on to the moment and they never wanted it to end.

CHAPTER SEVEN

At this point in the Funeral Mass, it was almost like the priest was talking to himself. Latin poured quietly from his mouth with his eyes opening and closing as he glanced at a large book in front of him.

Ms. Gussie Smith had come a long way walking from Eastend to downtown, St. Lawrence. But a walk from Eastend was nothing for most of them. The close proximity to downtown was one good thing about living in Eastend. For the most part, this is how they all got around.

Ms. Gussie looked up at the priest as he reverently performed the sign of the cross. She had no idea what was going on, but this was a funeral she would not have missed. Mae Mae was like the Queen of Eastend and she had to be here for her. That's just the way it was.

She had passed by this Catholic Church all her life, but never been through the doors until this day. But she knew very well that Mr. and Mrs. Brown, her 'White family' actually belonged to this church. And since, as they say, "Sunday is the most segregated day on earth," it was certainly a place where they would never have crossed paths.

But yes, Ms. Gussie was real close to the Browns. She had worked for them since she left high school. Her family had very little money to live on, so it was a sacrifice for her to leave school to help the family survive.

The Browns were like all of the other families that lived in Biltmore. They were like the other areas in Asheville where Negroes went to work for the very affluent White families. They loved their domestics just like family as long as they were at their homes working. But after the maids left and returned to their own side of the world, their employees knew little about how they lived and survived.

While the maids were entrusted with White employees' children and their grand possessions, these families knew little more than the names of several generations of Negro women who did their chores. They had little else in common other than a deep love for the children and pride in a home they could never have.

Ms. Gussie looked around and made a mental note of the other maids in the church. There was Ms. Minnie sitting there with her arms folded. Ms. Arabelle walked in alone and looked around like she was lost. Ms. Katie, Ms. Corrine, Ms. Helen and Ms. Gertrude all sat together on the same row dressed like a million dollars, even though they rode the bus and wore uniforms every day.

Looking at their strong determined faces, she knew they all worked hard every day of their lives. She knew they gave it their all even though no one ever seemed to care. She knew they all loved and admired Mae Mae because she'd never have to work as a maid.

Sunday's was the biggest meal at *Mae Mae's Eastend Café.* It was always in demand throughout the nearby community. Folks came through the front of the 'old school' slender doors that advertised RC cola and Colonial bread, in need of familiar home style cooking. Food had to be like 'Mama's' cooking. Like someone who cared cooked it. They could depend on Mae Mae's for that and much more.

Though Mae Mae allowed Big Jimmie to assist with the entrees on the other days, on Sunday's after church, she insisted they have only her special touch.

It was always the same menu, but the locals literally lined up for Sunday meals. Most of them ordered take-out but some loved the atmosphere of the Café so much they stayed to eat in. On the weekends, they sat around eating and shooting the bull just like one big family around the table.

Mae Mae dug in right after church. She started her potatoes first so that by the time the chicken finished frying she could tackle the potato salad. The collard greens had soaked in fat-back all morning.

Since Jimmie never attended church, he took care of the small preparations like the collards, the black-eyed peas, the sweet potatoes, rice and the vegetables of the day. The waitress, Bessie, arrived later in the afternoon to help with other demands.

Frying chicken for Mae Mae was an art. She seasoned her flour with just enough salt and pepper with a dab of paprika, heated the butter and Crisco oil in the black cast iron skillets to just the right temperature, and tested it with a flour covered wing.

Her secret was using a pad of pure butter in each pan while dipping the chicken in liquid egg whites before coating with flour and frying.

When she was sure of the temperature, she filled the pan with chicken touching on all sides. The chicken blood showed through the white flour, signaling the time it should be turned.

Piece after piece of crispy chicken was lifted from the pan and placed neatly aside to drain off excess grease. It was simply beautifully browned and though there was plenty, it was never enough. At *Mae Mae's Eastend Café* it was always first come, first served, especially on Sundays.

Her other main dishes included BBQ ribs and roast beef. These were seasoned and placed into the oven. For the oven cooked dishes, success was in the seasoning and waiting. They were so consistently prepared each and every Sunday that Mae Mae and her customers always knew what to expect. She could cook these meats with her eyes closed.

Though the food was always good, there were two strict rules on Sunday's. The first rule was, that only Gospel music was allowed to play on the juke box. The second rule was, Mae Mae was not to be disturbed while she was cooking. No matter what, no one, not even Esther, could talk to her. But her prey was always Jimmie.

"Boy! If you don't get that damned potato salad stirred up in the next two minutes I'm gonna jus' put yo' ass out o' the kitchen an' do it my damn self. You hear me?" she said, not even looking in his direction.

"It's coming! It's coming! Miss Mae", he said, not even flinching. He knew her threats and the more she cursed, even on Sunday, the lighter his sentence would be.

"You slow as molasses, Boy. You don't have nothin' to do but get the sides ready. I jus' don't know why I put up with yo' ass." It just wouldn't be the same if Mae Mae didn't fuss at Big Jimmie. In fact he expected it.

She dismissed any further need to harass him as she bent down to check the ribs in the oven. "Done," she said, more to herself than anyone else who might be listening.

The Sunday dinner crowd always arrived early. It was as if they knew they had very little weekend left to enjoy, so they wanted time to savor their food, their conversation and their friends. So at 4:30 on the dot, they started to arrive and order.

"Hey Ms. Mae. How you today?" Sapp shouted as he entered through the front double doors. "I'm gonna get mine to go today. Doris say she tired. So she soakin' her feet."

"OK, Sapp just go ova to da window an' let Bessie know what you want," she said, already knowing his story before he shared it.

The three front booths filled up soon after. The Mills family of five were regulars on Sunday. They walked down the hill from the top of Mountain Street and always got the fried chicken, rice and gravy and collards. That Jefferson couple from a block over, on Popular Street, sat down on the same side of the booth on the bench. He got the ribs and she got a vegetable plate.

Then Mr. Flynn was alone. He was married, but for whatever reason, he always came in alone and sat in the booth by himself. His large chicken breast, potato salad, and greens were always ready when he arrived at five o'clock. Somethings they just knew from experience, so why keep the customer waiting?

Once things began to settle down by six o'clock, Big Jimmie and Bessie took control of filling orders and serving while Mae Mae visited the tables to chat and to refill drinks.

She always sat down with Mr. Flynn to catch up on the latest news. As one of only a few Negro police officers in Asheville, he always knew what was happening.

"Hey Flynn," she said, with no particular fan fair. "What's been going on? I heard something was goin' on up the street at da' school las' night."

"Miss Mae! Miss Mae!" he said, with a big smile. "How in the world do you hear about every doggone thing before anybody else in Asheville?"

"Well," she said, smiling back and sitting down across from him in the booth. "You got ta unda' stan'. I'm in this place seven days a week and I end up seein' 'everybody and dey Mama' sometime or da otha. These folks just like talkin' to me, I guess."

"I know they do," Flynn said. "I fall into that trap myself. But ain't much goin' on. Those kids just vandalized the school up the way, that's all. They just got bored I guess. Broke out at lot o' windows, kicked some doors, and wrote on stuff. You know how they do. It's happened before."

"Who you think done it?"

"Who knows, Miss Mae. We never found 'em last time. But I suspect those bad ass kids over on Popular Street had something to do with it."

"Now why you say dat, Flynn? You ought not be blamin' dem boys if you don't know fa sho'."

"Yea you right. But those Lindsey boys and those Scott boys they hang with, is forever getting into stuff. They just haven't got caught yet, that's all. They dropped out of school and haven't got no jobs. Hanging out on the block, that's what they do. That's all they do. It's a matter of time and they are mine."

"Well, I'll keep my eyes and ears open. Dat's all I can do. I'd hate for those boys to get in trouble and go to jail if they didn't do nothin'."

"Miss Mae, you know I'm the kind of cop that wants the best for our kids. I want them to do well and get a good education and be somebody. But I have to do my job. I have to do what is expected especially when it comes to my own race.

If they do the crime and I find out they did, I will not hesitate to arrest them. I have to walk a thin line being a cop among my own people. It's not always easy."

"I understand," she said, shaking her head up and down. "These kids really need to see you wear a lot o' dif'rent hats. Some o' dem don't have no Daddies at home. Some got Mamas dat work all day from sun up ta sun down. So dey ain't neva home wit' dem. Dey need ta see men's can make it, jus' like you did. Dey need to see you pullin' fa dem ta do good."

"Yep, I know those things are important. I'd like to think I did a pretty good job with my son Michael. He just went off to A&T in Greensboro this fall. I miss him like crazy. He's me and Lula's only child, you know. But I always think about how blessed Michael was to have both of us. You know a Mama and a Daddy at home."

"Yep you so right. That sho' make a difference. Well, I gotta go now, Flynn," she said, as she stood up. "Jimmie and them pro'bly done burned down my kitchen."

He caught her before she walked away. "Oh, by the way, I meant to ask you, is Esther playing next weekend? I been working so hard, I missed the last couple of times."

"Sho' is! Dis Sa'day. Come on back by. Pork chops the special dat night too."

She retreated to the kitchen as the setting sun watched through the windows. Couples chatted in the booths satisfied with each other and the meal they'd long since completed. This was the quiet time after a busy day that they all needed prior to entering the other 'world' on Monday.

The kitchen was filled with dirty pots and dishes and the sounds of Mahalia Jackson's, "*Take my Hand Precious Lord.*" The rush was gone by the end of the day. As Mae Mae, Jimmie and Bessie cleaned the kitchen, there was a feeling of deep satisfaction.

The day was more than just ending, it was a comfortable yet quiet celebration. Each week they sensed a job well done, shown in the happy faces, the laughter and the empty plates. Words could not express this. So they cleaned in silence.

CHAPTER EIGHT

Davida Greene had all intentions of being on time to the funeral. But she ended up fighting to get through the downtown crowds as she walked to St. Lawrence from Eastend. Thank God the tall twenty year old was athletic and a tomboy of sorts.

She was darting in and out around people, trying her best to make it. She had no idea when she started out, that there was a parade going on today.

But November eleventh always brought with it Asheville's famous Veteran's Day parade. Most folks her age had no real desire to see old men in blue and gold baseball caps, waving American flags at the crowds as they rode by. But she spotted the Stephens Lee High School Marching Band performing and knew they were going to 'show out.'

Though she promised herself that she would not linger to watch, she couldn't help herself. Once she heard the loud rhythmic sounds of the Stephens Lee marching band, she had to watch.

She clapped and gloated as if every single band member was 'family.' The drum major looked like a giant. His height, the tall fury white hat, and the long gold baton he waved back and forth to the music, made him look like ten feet tall. There was no doubt, he was the star of the show. But the eight majorettes with a variety of beautiful brown complexions, shapely hips and thighs. Those things were emphasized by the short, tight uniforms, as strolled and marched like stars in their own right.

Davida followed them as they climbed Popular Street going toward downtown and suddenly into White America. David Millard Junior

High and the Winn Dixie were on the right side of the street, while the City Building, Courthouse and Post Office sat majestically on the left. These establishments ushered in Pack Square and Patton Avenue. As the band passed Woolworth, Bon Marche and Kress, Davida ran on in hopes of catching at least some of the funeral service.

The side door to the church was open so she just slid in quietly and sat in the back corner. From there she could see Mae Mae, but she could also see that all of Eastend had turned out for her.

Davida looked at the woman that she called her hero. She recalled that as a fifteen year old, she had entered Mae Mae's café hungry and asking for food. She will never forget how Mae Mae fed her and then told her she needed her to help out in the Café during her summer break.

Davida doubted how much she was actually needed in the Café. But hiring her at that age had kept her out of trouble, well fed and with pocket change. It was the nicest thing that anyone had ever done for her.

Eating meals at home was very strange for Mae Mae. For as long as she could remember, she usually had her meals at the Café. But now that she was no longer alone at the house, she had actually come to know her own kitchen. As much as she hated it, on Monday's, Big Jimmie was fully in charge of the Café. Good, bad or indifferent, Monday was her day off.

Mae Mae's beautiful house was built in 1958. It was right at the very top of Mountain Street looking over all of Eastend. The openness of the house let in beautiful rays of sunlight. It was furnished modestly, but the large dining room and kitchen, which was seldom used since her purchase two years ago, was the envy of the community.

She sat relaxing at the dining room table looking dreamily out of the window. On Monday mornings Esther cooked and waited on her. Looking up and smiling, Mae Mae breathed in the aromas of homemade biscuits, bacon and eggs. She smiled, thinking how nice it was being served for a change.

When she was finished and still sipping on her cup of coffee she said, "Baby we got to do somethin' with Little Jacob's head. Ya'll been goin' ova to Walton Street pool every day this week, and his hair lookin' a mess."

"Mama, you know his hair is really curly but I've been trying to keep it long and not cut it. He's got good hair, but it's just really thick. I think he got his hair gene more from you than from my Daddy. That Indian blood is way down the line," she said, as they both laughed. "But he loves to swim. He's doing really well too."

"Well just ask around at the café. Somebody at dat shop up on Eagle Street near the cab stand might can trim it. They say it's da bes' shop in town for cuts and fixin' women's hair too."

Esther thought long and hard. In her mind the barbershop/beauty parlor on Eagle near the cab stand, immediately translated into Mildred Jordan's shop. She knew that for Mae Mae, this small detail meant nothing. But for her, and her determination to move on in her feelings for Frank, seeing Mildred there in her shop, would be difficult if not impossible.

"Oh yeah, that's right," she said, as her mind flowed wildly and her emotions overwhelmed her. "I'm gonna think about that."

"The Pastor at St. James gits his cut there. You want me ta call him?"

"Yeah Mama, I guess so. See what you can find out."

The conversation ended just like it began. Out of nowhere the plans were made, and days later Esther and Little Jacob walked in to the Hipstyle Barbershop and Beauty Salon.

It was literally behind a row of idle cabs flanked by each driver taking care of his business. The establishment was right at the top of Eagle Street bordering much too closely with downtown Patton Avenue. Patton Avenue was almost another world. But there seemed to be an understanding, and the line of business dealings was seldom crossed.

Eagle Street and Patton Avenue were two streets that intersected, yet they were as different as night and day. Eagle Street was one strip of a super busy conglomeration of Negro owned businesses. Every type of business, both legal and not so legal, lined the streets on both sides.

This Eagle Street strip had everything a person could possibly want and need. The dirty streets and the rundown buildings carried fifty cent shots of liquor, clothes, shoe repair, hairdos or a good lay. All of this and much more was available for the right price on Eagle. It was a hub of Negro entrepreneurship. What made it so beautiful was the true opportunity for ownership. To own and 'run' something, was a freedom in itself.

Patton Avenue bragged of beautifully maintained department stores with perfect White manikins dressed in enviable dresses and suits. The street was clean and quiet, almost boring, compared to Eagle.

Well behaved Negroes could go inside the stores and businesses as long as they obeyed the recently and reluctantly removed signs that directed the races to the correct restrooms. Everything was in order and traffic flowed perfectly as cops on patrol were basically there for no more than decoration.

Esther held Jacob's hand tightly and they parked and walked toward the Hipstyle Barbershop and Beauty Salon. The people moving about on 'the block' were like them in many ways, but no one on Eagle was beyond a hustle. Basically Eagle Street was about business and was not to be confused with a day in the park.

"Hello everyone," Esther said politely, as she gently pushed Little Jacob through the door. "I'm Esther and this is my son, Jacob. We have a two o'clock appointment for a wash and trim with Ralph. Is he here?"

A very beautiful woman stood quickly and came forward with outstretched arms. She was short and shapely with gorgeous make-up and every hair in place.

"Esther, Esther! You don't remember me? I'm Mildred. We went to Stephens Lee together. But my God! Everybody knows who you are."

"Yes, Mildred, I remember" Esther said, trying her best to maintain some level of calmness. "You look good, Girl! You really do."

"Thank you so much, Honey. But anyway, Ralph's chair is right ova here. He'll take care of yo' cutie right away."

"Say hello to Mr. Ralph, Jacob," Esther said, trying to make him feel more comfortable.

It was difficult establishing that comfort level. Little Jacob did not know anyone in this strange place. And no one other than his Mama and Grandma Mae Mae had every done anything to his hair. This was his first haircut, and this 'hair thing,' was a new experience for them both.

Ralph sensed the unfamiliarity and gently took Little Jacob by the hand. He placed him in a riser seat, turned the chair to face him and just talked for a moment. For Ralph, this was not a time to rush.

"You ready to get handsome?" he said, with a welcoming smile.

"Yes!" Jacob said.

"Well, I promise not to hurt you, and when I'm done, you gonna be the best lookin' little dude in town. That sound good?"

"Yes" Jacob said, as he glanced at Esther moving away, seeing that her child was in great hands.

Esther seated herself in a small waiting area and picked up a 'Jet' magazine. As she flipped through the pages, she felt Mildred approaching.

"I just love the records you've put out Esther," Mildred said, out of nowhere. "I always knew that voice of yours would make you famous."

"Well thank you so much" Esther said, trying not to blush. "I had some good breaks. I guess you could say I ended up in the right place at the right time. That always helps."

They both laughed as Esther slipped away in thought while images of Frank with this beautiful creature exploded in her brain. A tinge of jealousy hit when all she could think about was the two of them making love.

"Frank use to talk about you all of the time. I have to say honestly, I got tired of hearing your name coming out of his mouth before we got married. I think he would have waited for you forever. But you know how us girls are when we see something we want," she said with a chuckle. "You was gone, and I wasn't about to let that handsome hunk get away."

"I understand," Esther said. "I would have done the same thing. Believe me."

When Ralph was finished, he turned Jacob around in a circle letting him model for Esther. The cutting and trimming, maybe even 'taming,' of his thick, curly hair looked wonderful.

"Oh, my little man!" Esther said. "You are so handsome. You ready to go show Grandma?"

As they gathered their things to say their goodbyes, Mildred excused herself from the customer in her chair to say goodbye. She hugged them as if they had been friends forever. And of course Esther returned the hug.

They then stepped into a sun lit afternoon. And as Saturday progressed on the outside, you could tell by the movement surrounding them, that Eagle Street 'the block,' was in preparation for a big night.

The weekends were filled with a variety of activities on 'the block.' But Esther could only think about getting back to Eastend to prepare for tonight's performance.

Each weekend, the crowds got bigger and bigger. Word had gotten around and now folks came to see her not only came from Eastend, but also Stumptown, Shiloh and Southside. *Mae Mae's Eastend Café* was the place to be for good food, good company and good entertainment.

The one spotlight above the stage hit Esther just right. The otherwise dim space showed clearly her light glowing bronze skin. She usually only smoked on stage, but when she did it became an intimate gesture. It connected her to her audience. It made them use all of their senses to know her better.

She finished her second song, took a long drag and blew it out slowly. Whatever she did on stage, she always took her time. There was no reason to rush. It was Saturday all over the world and none of them belonged to anyone on Saturday's.

"Ya'll like that?" she asked, in that sexy on stage voice. "That song, *'Knowing You is Loving You,'* is one of my favorites. I wrote it a while ago, up in New York. Back when I was young and in love," she said, followed by that sexy laugh.

"I hope you like this one too," she said, as she started to sing.

"Love unfinished, Love unproved. Look in my eyes and see I'm moved. Here then gone. But now alone. I see you, Baby. Baby, I see you. Is it love? Does love hurt like this? Is it really? Love unfinished, Love unproved. Look into my heart. Look into my mind. Can you see? Why can't you see?"

It was clearly a conversation. It was something that needed to be said yet could only be said in a song. It was raw emotions that were felt by all but had to be expressed by someone's soul. It was a love letter where love could not be denied, but it had to be.

"Oh my God!" she said. "That takes us way back, don't it? Just hang out with me, ya'll. Hang out with me and you don't know what you gonna go home to. You might end up doin' some thangs tonight you haven't done in a real long time," she said with a chuckle.

Everyone in the room was of one mind. In that time and in that place it became an entire room of people in love with everyone around them. Just in that moment, not before and not after, she had brought them to love something, someone, somewhere, sometime. She controlled pure love.

When it was over, Esther retreated into herself. Like making love and needing to find personal meaning physically, mentally, emotionally, she broke away. She had given her all and could not be expected to give anything more. She was spent.

Her back booth in the dark awaited her. It was her cave, her place where she could exist but hide from those who yearned to know her insides. She owed them nothing else, and since they were satisfied completely, they expected nothing else.

"Hey Esther," it was that voice again. "Just dropping in. Hope you don't mind."

"Frank," she said, surprised to see him. "I didn't expect to see you this evening. What's up? Please, please have a seat."

"I wanted to talk to you," he said. "I was hoping you'd go with me to a place where we could talk, some place away from here."

"Wow! What kind o' talkin' you need to do?" she said smiling.

"I just have a lot on my mind," he said. "If it's not possible, I understand."

"No. I just need to change clothes and make sure Mama can got home in time to be with Jacob. Where did you have in mind?"

"You heard of the *Skyland Club* up on the mountain? It's always nice and quiet."

"OK, just pick me up at Mama's in about an hour. I'll change and kiss my Baby goodnight and then we can go."

"Sounds good."

Frank arrived at the house and she didn't invite him in but stepped out to meet him just as he rang the doorbell. The moon shown above them as they drove silently, not knowing what awaited them. The night was perfect as the stars glistened providing a special light that highlighted their two beautiful profiles.

When they arrived, Esther observed that the *Skyland Club* was just like being in another world. They were met at the car with no choice but to valet park. Once the car was out of sight, they were met by a doorman who clearly had seen Frank many times before and knew him well. She also noticed that the only color this club saw was green. That was obvious by the way everyone was treated.

"Mr. Jordan," the short, dark, uniformed man said with a big smile. "May I help you this evening?"

"We'll be going to the private dining room tonight," Frank said. "Let's just start there."

The doorman smiled and escorted them to a semi-private area with other couples chatting quietly in dim light. He seated them almost knowing where Frank wanted to be. After receiving his tip, he disappeared.

"Sorry that this was so last minute," Frank said, apologetically. "So much was going on that you didn't even realize. I just had to talk to you."

"Ok," she said, with a question still lingering in the air.

"Well let me just cut out all of the drama and get to what's on my mind." He breathed in deeply and began.

"Esther, I understand you were in Mildred's shop the other day. She came home and was about to burst. She couldn't wait to tell me about it. She said you all were very cordial."

"Yes," she said. "How else would we be but cordial?"

"To tell you the truth, Esther, I can't understand why of all places in Asheville, you just had to go to *Hipstyle Barbershop and Beauty Salon*. Did you know that was Mildred's shop?"

"Yes, Mama said that was her shop."

"I just don't get it, Esther. You know I love you. I never got over you. Mildred knows it too. And as I try to sort it all out, she comes home and says, 'Frank, you'll never know who I saw at the shop today.'

"Ever since I saw you in Eastend and up on that stage, it triggered something in me that I thought I was over. But I'm not over you, Esther. Sadly my emotions are so all over the place right now that I don't know what to do. And knowing that you and Mildred were face to face just didn't help matters. God! Why did you go there, Esther? Why?"

"Wow!" she said, in a low, thoughtful tone. "I thought twice about it. But I never thought it would affect you like this. It was all very innocent. She greeted me like a long lost friend. Jacob got his hair cut. And we said goodbye."

"Nothing regarding us has ever been innocent, Esther. And regardless of how Mildred greeted you, she knows it. She has feared you and your return the whole time she and I have been married. She knew that even though you were miles away, she was sharing me with you.

72

"Your return has been bitter sweet, Esther. My heart longs for you but my mind fears the hurt it will cause. God! I want you so bad. I just can't stand it."

They sat in silence for a time that both of them needed. It was necessary too for their heads to attempt to catch up with their emotions. Esther finally broke the silence. Knowing that even though her usual way was always to avoid emotions, she felt this seemed like the time in life when emotions were vital.

"Frank," she said softly, looking deeply into his eyes. "All I know is, I don't want to talk any longer. Right now, I just want desperately to be in your arms."

"Give me a moment," he said urgently, as he left the table.

He approached the doorman and whispered something in his ear. Before Esther knew it, she found herself in an elegantly decorated room that was one of several rooms tucked deeply away toward the rear of the club. It was so high on the mountain that when they looked out of the window, every light of Asheville shined back at them like extra stars in the sky.

Love that had been on hold for much too long flooded the room. An urgency that was way beyond their control took over. They moaned in unison in a language only understood by them and only at this moment, in this time and space.

This was not at all about fulfilling a sexual desire. It was about the pure unadulterated unity of two human beings who were meant to be together.

No words could describe it. So no words were expressed.

Frank took her slowly, as if savoring every moment, as if taking the lost time he deserved. He looked into her eyes and touched her soft skin. He kissed her beautiful lips endlessly, searching deeply with his tongue into her very soul.

Esther had never experienced this level of love making ever before in her life. She was on another planet, in another world and wishing never to return to earth. Reaching down she felt his hardness and that sensation took her to another realm. Her height of passion was in unfamiliar but welcome territory.

Unlike any other time and with any other person, this act was pure and natural and right. Their bodies existed only for each other. Their minds, their souls rediscovered the reason they never ever loved another human this same way.

Like a ballet beautifully performed, yet never rehearsed, they instinctively knew their roles. He rolled to his back allowing her dominance that he knew she deserved. She graciously accepted while rewarding him with kisses to his lips and neck while straddling him. Her movements were slow yet calculated, as she attempted to feel everything possible while simultaneously giving everything totally to him.

Nothing was forced and as she moved, they fit together perfectly. The time, the place, the people, the moment could never be captured in the same way again. Their eyes met as she touched his face and went deeper into him. At that moment they moaned uncontrollably and climaxed together.

CHAPTER NINE

The church seemed more alive as they all listened to the booming cacophony of the organ. Each individual pipe that was displayed on high at the front, seemed to know its own purpose. The song was unknown and totally foreign to them, but the majestic sound it released into the air was a welcome tribute.

The priest sat with his head down, relieved that the part he played would soon be over. He was flanked by altar boys seated on both sides who seemed to feel the same way. All of them including the priest were there out of duty and not necessarily to honor the unknown person in the casket before them.

Mrs. Geldman glanced up at the priest silently impatient as she also waited for an end to it all. A Catholic church was the last place she wanted to be, but Mae Mae had been a loyal customer at her store for ages. An even though she was Jewish, supporting her friend at this time of loss was very important.

Geldman's Store was right in the center of these folk's world. It was at the bottom of Eagle Street, which intersected with Valley Street and the dirt road called Dirty Eagle.

Still on the outskirts of Eastend, the store could not have been placed in a more segregated area. But somehow this Jewish family had long since discovered that the color of money was the same no matter what area or whose hand it came from.

Based on the theory of supply and demand, the store and the owners fit perfectly in this community. No one seemed to care that a Jewish family was right there among them, providing exactly whatever goods they needed.

It didn't seem to matter that other Whites seldom drove along Valley Street and would not be caught dead around Eagle Street. Yet, the Geldman's were a part of the community and they knew their customers very well.

Mrs. Geldman was a fifty-something, attractive woman with dyed blond hair and lots of make-up. And though she and her husband worked in their own store, behind the counter, with no outside help, today she looked really classy. Her brown cashmere jacket, and matching suede shoes looked nothing like the white apron and flats she wore every day at the store.

They had come to feel very comfortable in their work environment. But regardless of how well they fit in at the store, they locked up and left Eastend before sundown each day. They left this poor community and went to their own wealthy area until the next day. Though wealthy, their own neighborhood where Jews were allowed to purchase in Asheville, was segregated too.

But here at St. Lawrence, for more reasons than one, she felt very out of place. She was in another world, just like every single day of her life. As the altar boy knelt down and rang the little bell beside him, she jerked to attention. She looked at her watch, sat way back in the pew and rested her foot on the padded kneeler in front of her.

The Saturday night special at Mae Mae's Café *was* fried pork chops, rice and gravy, string beans and biscuits. Beer and shots along with good food, good music and dancing served as a great escape.

This was the place for anybody who was anybody in Eastend to be on a Saturday night. After spending all week in a world where they didn't belong, and owned nothing or had nothing, on Saturdays the Eastend crowd came back home. They could let down their hair and be themselves, be somebody, anybody.

When the clock struck nine and everyone had their fill of food, the beer and shots began to roll. Around 'family' there were no inhibitions, no reason to hide, and no reason to be timid. Everyone already knew their role and their lines in the continuing drama.

Mack was feeling good as the whiskey shots were kicking in. He approached Irma, politely turned his back to her, and put out his hand behind him. This was his signal that he wanted to dance.

The record was slow. '*Wonderful World*' by Sam Cook, filled the dance floor. Mack and Irma led the way, went to the center of the floor and held each other so tightly that no space was visible between them.

They all did a one-step grind, in beat but barely moving. The movement, the intimacy was very familiar regardless of who the partners might be. It was all a part of the dance.

Before the record was barely over, the slow and sensual groove changed as quickly as the records flipping in the juke box. Now they danced to Chubby Checker's *'The Twist.'* The slow dancers simply let go of one another, moved back and began to dance and sing. *"Come on Baby and do the twist. Come on Baa-by, and do the twist."*

They sang and laughed and moved like there was no tomorrow. And when it was over, they went their separate ways and sat down. The drinks were there, the gossip was there, and joy was all around them.

They were up and down all night long. Listening to *'Will Love You Tomorrow,'* by the Shirelles, *'Chain Gang' and 'You Send Me,'* by Sam Cook, *'Tutti Frutii,' 'Lucille,'* and *'Good Golly Miss Molly,'* by Little Richard.

For the Eastend crowd, good music was good music, they didn't care what the artists looked like. They also danced to the sounds of Ricky Nelson, Buddy Holly and Elvis.

By eleven, things were slowing down and some folks were making decisions about where they would finish the evening. Sometimes the slow dance grind got too good to just leave at Mae Mae's Café and go home. Sometimes it ended up in somebody's bedroom. But it was for this evening and this evening only. And if it happened, it wasn't nobody else's business.

As usual, when things began to quiet down, Mae Mae left the work to Big Jimmie and Bessie and sat at the bar to relax. Wallace, the tall and dark former Stephens Lee quarterback, whose wife had been missing this evening, approached her.

"Hey Mizz Mae," he said, sitting on the stool next to her. "How you doin' this evenin'?"

"Hey Wallace, she said. "I'm fine. Where yo' wife at, Boy?" she said, laughing. "I saw you an' Regina ova dere in dat corner dancin'."

He laughed knowing that nothing ever got passed Mae Mae in her Café. "Oh you know I wasn't doin' nothin', Mizz Mae. A little dancin' ain't never hurt a thang."

"Yep!" She said in agreement. "Those double doors to dis Café been holdin' in people's secrets for a long time. Ain't nothing,' neva goin' outta here. Don't worry."

I know, Mizz Mae. Hey, you heard about all that stuff been happenin' in Greensboro finally paid off today?"

"What stuff?"

"You know, for months dey been at the Woolworths at dat lunch counter refusin' to leave 'til dey got served. Well, today dey got served. Dis day, July 24, 1960, goin' down in history."

"Hallelluyah!" she said. "Lord knows thangs been needin' to change for a long time. Thank you Jesus!"

"Yep. Since those boys from A & T first sat down back in February, lots o' Colored folks been sittin' in and going to jail riskin' they lives to change thangs. An' now that movement's goin' all over the South. It just took standin' up for our rights, Mizz Mae."

"Well, da worl' gone git betta. Peoples gonna get along betta an' maybe we'll all live side by side."

"Mizz Mae, don't get too excited. We got a long way ta go. They don't even want us ta go to school together. We got Stephens Lee and they got Lee Edwards High and never to two shall meet.

Sometimes I think about how it might have been for me to play football at that White school. Wonder if I could've got some scholarships and maybe played in da pros."

"I know it's been slow, Baby. But maybe by da time my grandchild get olda, thangs might be a whole lot betta."

Both of them sat silently for the next few moments. They realized that times were changing. They had no idea how, when or to what degree. They just knew that every single person would have to play a part.

CHAPTER TEN

Big Jimmie looked around, embarrassed that Mae Mae was signaling him to the front of the church. She was dramatically insisting that he get up there and sit with the family. So with his tail between his legs, he as usual, did just as she said.

He was self-conscious about his weight everywhere except in the MaeMae's Eastend Café. He knew that in the Café, he was the king. Next to Mae Mae, no one could run that place, including handle to cooking, like he could. This had been his place of refuge for ages. It was the place he could go and be somebody. He could do what he enjoyed. He could be in the mix of things.

Though it appeared to everyone that Big Jimmie constantly took a verbal beating from Mae Mae, Jimmie didn't care. She cursed him up one side and down the other and ordered him around like a slave master, but he still loved her like a mother. In fact he would think something was wrong, if she didn't treat him this way.

Truth is, Big Jimmie never finished high school. He couldn't take the teasing that continued endlessly from the time he entered first grade. By ninth grade, he still could not read and write.

But whenever he cut school and ended up at the Café crying at the back door, Mae Mae always let him come in. She tried to convince him to go back and at least try to get a good education, but for him, the hurt and pain was always too much.

Big Jimmie was basically an orphan raised by a 'sometimes off and sometimes on' Grandma on Velvet Street. He never knew love from an adult in his life until he met Mae Mae. She always thought being hard and firm with him in addition to showing love was what he needed to develop into a strong man. What little he'd learned about being a man, he learned from Mae Mae, the matriarch in his life.

Sometimes he reminded Mae Mae too much of old evil Red, the most hated person in her entire life. But after she looked passed the fat body, light skin and bright brown eyes, the soft, loving, shy Jimmie appeared.

She knew he just needed love and guidance and she was determined to give him all that she could. Jimmie was more than someone who worked for her. He was a part of her family.

It was Monday night and Esther knew Mae Mae would be home from the Café. As usual, she cooked a meal that her mother never would have taken the time to eat at the Café. Tonight it was T-bone steak, baked potato, and fried green tomatoes.

As she took the steak out of the oven, she placed it on the large plate beside the other food. Mae Mae loved these times, when like no other, she was catered to. She gladly received her full plate and without missing a beat, cut into her medium well steak.

Esther sat down at the table, but did not prepare a plate for herself. With her chin in hand and elbows on the table, Mae Mae knew that something was on her mind.

"Well, Baby Doll," Mae Mae said, between bites, "Spit it out! I know you, an' you got somethin' goin' on in yo' head. What's up?"

"You're right, Mama. You do know me like a book," Esther said. "I was wondering if you could keep Jacob tonight. You know he wasn't feeling well and went to bed early, but I wanted to step out if you don't mind."

Mae Mae put her fork down and finished the bite she had in her mouth before she commented. She had waited patiently for this conversation for a long time.

"You know I ain't neva got no problem wit' keepin' my Gran'Baby," she said. "But we both know dat ain't da problem. I'm yo' Mama chil' an' I see everything. When was you gone tell me you was seein' Frank Jordan?"

"It's not something I'm proud of Mama. It just happened and at this point neither one of us know what to do."

"Honey, you know dat man got a wife and a child. Have you thought about what it might do ta dem? Do you want to be a home wrecka? Don't you care 'bout dem innocent people, Esther? "

"I do care Mama, an' I tried. I promise you. I tried to tell him, that was it. But Mama, I haven't ever loved another human being like I love Frank."

"Well, my motherly advice to you both is this. If ya'll all dat hot for each other like it's eternal love, somebody need to tell dat woman. Don't have that woman findin' out da wrong way. You hear?"

"Yes Mama. I hear you. Frank keeps saying he wants a divorce from Mildred. And I just don't know what to do. My dream is to live happily ever after with him, but I just hate to hurt so many people."

"Well go ahead and go out. Jus' be careful."

The last few months, Frank and Esther had become regulars at the *Sky Club*. Both of them knew very well the consequences of their actions. But as soon as their eyes met, they always knew there was no turning back. The pure attraction and the true love they felt when they were together, was much too strong to resist.

"Hello," she said, rolling down the window as she drove up beside him outside.

His smile widened as he noticed she was dressed exactly the way he liked. All white linen, highlighted her beautiful complexion. The cool material blew in a slight wind, showing her perfect butt and round breasts.

"How are you?" he said, with a smiling sexy tone that hung in the air.

"Now, I'm much better," she said, still smiling too.

"I'd like to treat you to a drink, and maybe a few other things," he said, opening her door and helping her get out.

They both laughed, as loud, fun, haughty laughs took them up the stairs to the entrance. They went into the dimly lit lounge and sat in the plush, comfortable chairs. Other well-dressed couples were at discretely placed at tables around them, but it was as if they were alone. They were the only people in the world.

"I've missed you," she said, leaning in, whispering in his ear.

"I missed you too, Baby. Believe me, it's getting harder and harder to live without you. I don't know how long I can pull this off. You know, us just meeting like this."

"I know. Mama questioned me tonight. And she knows about us, Frank. I could never fool her."

"And God knows Mildred is wondering what's going on. I haven't touched her since you and I made love, Esther. I can't think of anyone but you."

They sat in silence conflicted by the drastic need they had and all of the people they could hurt. What could they do? What should they do? These questions swirled around them as they got up and headed to the room. It was like paradise awaited them, but the only way they could have it was to walk through the burning sands.

In silence, they undressed one another slowly, as their eyes never lost sight of each other. They took this night slower than usual, holding on, caressing and kissing. He kissed her lips lightly feeling the softness, the heat, the wetness.

He took her face in both of his hands and wanted to see her soul through her eyes. His hands slowly, deliberately touched every part of her body. The desire overwhelmed him as he wanted to know her through the sense of touch alone.

Esther enjoyed his touching, but all she could think of was how desperately she wanted him inside her. Her mind could only see them becoming one. She could not resist him for another minute, as she took full control and climbed on top of him.

The power, the control was in her hands as he danced to her lead. And all the while he could care less as he enjoyed each thrust.

Exhaustion approached just in time as they erupted in unison and held on tight. The shadows of their souls stood in the air over them, not wanting it to end. But it always did.

Moments passed, then Frank broke the silence. "What we gone do, Baby?"

Esther ignored the question which weighed heavily on each of their minds. She simply held him tightly and started to sing.

"You can tell my love is deep by how I move with you. By how I grove with you. You can tell. Just the touch of your hand brings me close to you. Oh so close to you. And I scream for you every time. So can't you tell? Baby can't you tell?"

When the words ended, she put her lips close to his ear and just hummed. This became a momentary escape from the pain their love was causing.

"I know this is a subject you never wanted to talk about," Frank said. "But we must. No matter how we look at it, people we love will be hurt and won't understand."

"My God! Frank. This is just too hard. As much as I hate it. We just have to grow up. Let's just stop seeing each other. Let's end it tonight! OK?"

"No Esther," he said. "That's not an option. Lord only knows, I can't live without you. I won't do that again. I plan to ask for a divorce from Mildred. It's the only choice I have."

The view down the mountain of Asheville was highlighted by a bright full moon. It was usually a beautiful sight. But tonight as they struggled with the biggest decision of their lives, the moon looked on them in judgement.

"When do you plan to tell her, Frank?" she asked, in a low sad tone.

"Soon. That's all I can say. Soon."

CHAPTER ELEVEN

All heads turned as he walked into the church unusually late with a loud thud, a stench and an unkempt appearance, like no other visitor present. 'Pipe Daddy,' as he was known in Eastend, could care less if everyone stared at him. He was used to it anyway. People had looked at him like that most of his adult life.

But like most of the Eastend folks at the church, he was there for Mae Mae. There wasn't another person in Asheville that could draw him this far downtown and out of his element, but her.

'Pipe Daddy' was the only name people knew. And though no one could tell you his real name, all of them knew him. He was like a fictional character with built in props.

It was hard to tell his true complexion because of the years of dirt and black dust from working in the coal yard. Though well into his late fifties, handling coal had made him fit. One thing was always certain, a pipe was either in his hand or hanging from his mouth. It was held between dark brown and missing teeth.

Most of the time people saw 'Pipe Daddy' when he was delivering coal. Today however, just for Mae Mae, he attempted to clean himself up. But the overalls that used to be blue and the green faded shirt were still worn and dirty.

He had not bathed in a long while and his coal faded black hands would never be clean again. The railroad cap he always wore was missing. Today, just for Mae Mae, he had removed it.

Coughing loudly and deeply, he looked around as he took his seat. Several familiar faces looked back at him. He had delivered coal for years to many folks in the Eastend crowd present in the church. Coal, just like 'Pipe Daddy,' was black and dirty. But both were the poor man's friend during the cold Asheville winters.

The *Hipstyle Barbershop and Beauty Salon* was Mildred's pride and joy. And because of it, life was good. It was always good. Or maybe the kids like her who grew up in Lee Walker Heights, Asheville's first 'projects,' didn't know any different.

Their's was the era of being poor but happy. It was a time when parents worked hard and loved their kids so deeply that they all believed they were rich.

But Mildred was on top of the world. It seemed as though most everything in life she wanted, she ultimately got it. She got Frank Jordan; she owned her own beauty shop; and she lived in Asheville's Negro suburbs in a fabulous home. But most of all, she had Jack. She had her child with Frank Jordan and he was the glue that held her questionable marriage together. She was the luckiest girl in the world.

Mildred loved her shop and her patrons. But it was sometimes a real chore to pull herself away from her nice neighborhood in exchange for the other world of Eagle Street. It was the fast life. For the movers, the groovers, the business owners like her, it was the good life. There was an indescribable atmosphere that was a drawing card for most of their community.

"Good morning, Ya'll," she shouted, as she entered the door and immediately grabbed her white smock. "How ya'll doin' today?"

"Fine," Ralph said. "An' you?"

"I'm ok," said Ms. Delia, much quieter than usual.

"Well, I got three heads today and then I'm gone leave ya'll with it. It's Saturday an' I'm gonna do somethin' special wit' my man tonight. We haven't been out together in ages, and out of the blue this morning, he wanted to go to dinner.

Ralph and Miss Delia glanced at each other, but said nothing. It was getting harder every day to be in the shop and pretend they knew nothing was going on. But how do you tell someone you love just like a sister, that her man was now somebody else's man.

"Why ya'll so quiet this mornin'?" she asked, looking at them over the glasses she only wore in the shop.

"Nothin'. We solid, we good," they said almost in unison.

"Delia, I need you to give me a touch up and do my eyebrows," Mildred cut in. "You gone have time? I'm gonna look fly tonight. You hear me?"

Throughout the day there was a cloud over the others in the shop. But Mildred's private sun was so bright that she could not see the rest of the world. So, as if on cloud nine, she finished her last head, saw the customer out, gathered her things and said goodbye.

Eagle Street was gearing up for another wild and busy Saturday night. But tonight she was going far away from there and into her other world with her husband. Her eyebrows were neatly arched, and her hair was styled perfectly. All she needed to do was drive to Shiloh, dress and wait for Frank.

Frank arrived home shortly after Mildred. She knew it was truly a sacrifice for him to be with her on a Saturday night because it was his busiest day on 'the block.' "So perhaps he needed this time as much as she did," she thought. Maybe he missed these special occasions just as she had."

"Hey, what's up? he asked, entering the side door, from the garage. "You don't mind if we just go grab a bite to eat do you? I'm not up for nothin' else tonight. Sorry."

Mildred tried to sustain the smile that had been on her face all day, but her heart sank. Her bubble burst, as she slowly let go of her expectations for a romantic evening of dining and dancing and hanging out with the man she loved.

"That's fine," she said.

She noticed that he didn't even bother to freshen up or change clothes. He found Jack in his room coloring with the baby sitter. He hugged him much more tenderly than usual, and then he was ready to go.

They entered the small restaurant near the Westgate Shopping Center. Frank had few choices since *Mae Mae's Eastend Café* wouldn't work and *The Sky Club* was out of the question. Nice places to go and eat good food were few and far between during these times of semi-segregation. But after a short wait, they were seated near the back.

"You look nice tonight." Frank said, as he looked at the menu, and not at her.

"Thank you. I wanted this to be a special evening for us," she said. "We haven't gone out in a long time."

"I know. Both of us just stay so busy. But I have something I needed to talk to you about tonight anyway. Let's order first. You know what you gonna have?"

"Wow! You not waistin' no time, are you?" she said, sarcastically. "I know what I want to eat. But what's goin' on wit' you. You're actin' real strange."

The waitress stood above them impatiently, chewing gum as she waited for their orders. Once they ordered, she took the menus and left.

"So what's so important you got to talk about so bad?" Mildred asked. "You got my curiosity up."

"Believe me, this is not easy, Mildred," Frank said, nervous, but happy for an opening.

"Well, you know I love you like my best friend, but I've never been in love with you. Right?"

"What in the hell you talkin' about, Frank? What is it you tryin' to say?"

The food was brought to the table before he could answer. Frank dug in to grilled chicken, corn on the cob and collards. Mildred ate slowly and quietly as she showed little interest in her fried fish, cole slaw and fries.

"Mildred I can't live the lie that I've been living. I can't go another moment without telling you the truth. I started seeing Esther shortly after she came back to town.

"Believe me we both tried to resist it. We didn't want to hurt anyone, especially you. But, the more she and I are together, the more we realize how much we're still in love with each other."

Mildred sat still and quiet like a volcano before a major eruption. Her voice said nothing, but her body and her eyes spoke volumes. When she began, she shouted at the top of her voice.

"I should have known," she said, with tears flooding her eyes. "It was just a matter of time. I knew you just had to have her. Well, don't even think I'm gonna give you a divorce. I ain't gone make it easy for ya'll, Frank. I can promise you that!

"And don't even think about going any place and taking Jack. That's out of the question.

"Yeah! You come talkin' about how we the best o' friends an' that's all. Well, Honey you sho' as hell wasn't callin' me friend when you was fuckin' me every chance you got."

"Mildred!" Frank said, as he held up his hand in hopes of quieting her. "Please keep your voice down!"

Hearing her speak of Jack, his pride and joy, at that volume scared Frank back to reality. With his child's name flooding from her mouth in the midst of threats and profanity, he knew having Esther would not be easy.

"Wait a minute now, Mildred," he said, with an air of retreat in his voice. "Why you have to bring Jack into this? You know I will never just leave my son with you."

"Well, damn it! You best decide which one you want the most. That Bitch or yo' son. 'Cause I ain't goin' nowhere.

"I ain't never really had you noway. I might have been yo' wife and yo' business partner. But you ain't never loved me. So I'm just fine with you havin' yo' outside Bitch and then comin' home to me a Jack. I just refuse to give you and my good life up."

Steaming from the inside out, she was quiet for a brief moment. Then she spoke with a smile that meant nothing to either of them.

"That's right! That's what we'll do. You have her, if that's what you want. You just be discrete and make sure you remember where home is. Yeah! You work it that way if you just got to have her."

Frank thought for a long moment. What Mildred described would be fine for any old woman he just wanted to get next to in bed. But this would never work for him and Esther. He had waited his whole life to be with Esther.

"Tell you what, Mildred, let's just let all of this digest for a little while. Don't make any drastic moves yet. Just cool it for a minute."

"That's fine," she said, with a lower tone. "Cause, like I said, I ain't goin nowhere."

The waitress appeared at the table right on cue, as they sat in silence. "Ya'll want dessert?" she asked, not even noticing the cold chill around the table.

"No. That will be all. I'll take the check," Frank said, hoping no one else in the room had heard their conversation.

The ride home was painful for them both as they pondered silently how their lives were about to change. Frank glanced over as he sat at the traffic light. The person who had been his best friend and the mother of his child was hurting. And not only was he the cause of that pain, he could do nothing to stop it. Love and pain are so much closer than he ever thought or knew.

He parked the car and they both walked in. As he reached the bottom of the stairs, Frank raced up to the top, almost frantically. All he wanted to do at this time, at this moment, was to see Jack.

CHAPTER TWELVE

Mae Mae always said Gregory was going to be the President of the United States one day. Of course it was always said with a chuckle. Everyone knew there was no way in hell a Negro would ever be able to attain the highest office in the land. But every time Gregory came into the Café, she'd say it over and over again, laughing all the time.

So if nothing else, that crazy talk of hers at least made him dream big. Gregory was an 'A' student and was soon to graduate from Morehouse College in Atlanta.

Mae Mae knew he was smart as a whip. And if she didn't tell him how smart he was, who would? That's how she was. Ms. Mae looked deeply into the heart and soul of every person that entered through the double doors of her Café. And when she looked, she always found something unique about each and every person. In Gregory, she saw a smart, successful young man.

He smiled as he looked towards her up at the front of the church. He couldn't wait to tell her that he had been close enough to shake the hand of Martin Luther King Jr. and had even marched with him.

Dr. King and his non-violent protests had begun to spread like wild fire among the students at Morehouse and Spelman, as well as all across the country. Students like Gregory felt empowered by a leader like Dr. King to peacefully do whatever it took to improve the human rights for all mankind, especially African Americans.

"Yep! I came today knowing Ms. Mae's loss and knowing how proud she would be. I wanted to tell her that I was right there at the Lincoln Memorial when Dr. Martin Luther King, Jr. made his 'I Have a Dream Speech.'

"Students from colleges all over the globe were there to hear that speech and to stand in solitude with him. It was all about racial harmony and Human Rights. The way Dr. King delivered that speech, maybe I could be President."

"Mizz Mae, Mama Peggy wanted me to come and tell you that she couldn't thank you enough for doin' this special thang tonight fa' Beverly Ann."

"Oh Honey," Mae Mae said, in her matronly tone. "Ya'll know I'm here fa ya'll. Didn't nobody know dat chile was gone get dat sick, dat fast. An' everybody in Eastend so sorry dat baby died."

"Yes Mam' dey say she passed cause her appendix busted. Chile won't but nine years old. But it hit Mama Peggy hard. It's just hard to believe how a young chile die way before dey even lived."

"I know," Mae Mae said. "Ya'll's family been in Eastend up on Mountain Street fo'eva. I jus' wanna help howeva I can. Esther gone get out there tonight an' do a show and I'm plannin' a fish fry. We gone give everythang we make to pay fa dat chile's funeral."

"Well Mama Peggy, she say 'thank you.' But she ain't gone come out though. She just too torn up ova all dis."

"I know, Baby. I know."

Friday was always a great time to party. It was the end of a hard work week and a couple of days before going back for a repeat. And to have Esther on stage, liquor in hand and the smell of fried fish coming from Mae Mae's kitchen, it was something special.

The occasion was not one for celebration, but Eastend would turn out for the opportunity to support, party, give back and enjoy themselves all at the same time.

Esther's show was starting in about an hour, at nine on the dot. So everyone arrived at the Café at around seven, ate and danced and partied waiting around for Esther to appear.

But on a Friday, that fried fish was in a category of its own. It was fried to perfection because Big Jimmie fried the fish. And he had a way of frying it with just the right combination of egg dip and meal, that the crispiness was unbelievable. It was fried fish that everyone already knew melted in your mouth. You could not get this taste anywhere else in the entire city of Asheville.

Right at nine, Esther appeared on stage. She was absolutely beautiful. She wore all white. From head to toe white popped out and greeted the audience like, 'OK, here I am.' It commanded the mood whether they wanted it or not.

They all looked at her and waited. They wanted her to take them away. They waited for her to take them to a place that remembered and paid homage to Beverly Ann. But they also wished to go to a place of their own. The community needed to morn together, yet party together. They needed to feel, yet be filled. They needed to come together, yet go inside of themselves.

Esther entered the stage to applause. Applause was like money that you could not touch or cash in. It was personal. It paid the heart and soul in a way that could never be taken to the bank. But Esther loved every minute of it. It helped her to give her all and more when she performed.

"Hello my Loves," she said. "I am so glad you are here with me tonight. My God!" she said loudly. "We are here for the family that has lost a young loved one. We're here tonight for Beverly Ann. She was young. She was innocent. And she was called by the Lord."

She lit a cigarette and took the time it takes to expel every stream of smoke into the air. It was as if she owned time. Like every moment was bought and paid for by her. She would not be rushed for anyone. Then she finally spoke, again.

"Loves," she said. "Our hearts are hurting for our child that went on to be with the Lord. But let us rejoice this evening. Let's give our hearts and souls to Beverly Ann while we rejoice that she is now sitting on the lap of our Lord."

They applauded loudly. They needed to be directed to peace in a time when understanding was lacking. They needed to know that even though the loss of this young soul was upon them, it was God's will.

"I have a song I want to share tonight. I know that we all have had a time of tears. When tears flowed from our eyes and we couldn't help it. When we had a loss that could not be explained.

When we recognize that God is in control and not us. But remember that tears come without invitation. They come invited only by the heart."

The lights were low. Everyone was full of good food and cooling out on bourbon and gin as they listened to every word. The mood was perfect as she began to sing.

"Tears from inside out, they flow. Uncontrolled. Unchecked. Tears, I want to hide them, to protect them from enemy eyes. Tears. They have no color, no gender, no kindship. They just come and then disappear into the palms of my hands and recycle for the next time."

Esther sang from the heart as that level, that depth was what everyone needed from her. In the darkness of the room, they all went to another place. They dove into her words, into the general mood, and into the reason they were all there. Mourning a young girl gone way before her time, made more sense to the rhythmic beat and smooth voice singing a song.

"I love that song" she said. "It's alright to cry, ya'll. Time passed fast. Then Esther flirted with the audience during several other songs, and said good night.

"Mama, I'm so sorry about that child passing away. I hope my show was good and we made a lot of money to help out," Esther said to Mae Mae, looking up from her favorite booth.

"Yes, Honey," Mae Mae said. "It was a good night. I think Miss Peggy gone have what she need to put that child away nice. Thanks to you for doin' the show tonight instead of Saturday night. I think that brought out mo' numba's."

"Oh, no problem. I can't imagine losin' a child that young. If that ever happened to Jacob, they'd have put me under the grave."

Moments passed and silence grew between them. Then out of nowhere, Mae Mae posed the question she'd been wanting to ask for a long time.

"So, we haven't talked in a while," Mae Mae said, changing the subject. "What you finally decide to do about Frank Jordan?"

Silence again. It was a subject that both of them knew would continue to surface. It was a subject the mother and daughter could not avoid for much longer.

"I don't know, Mama. We've talked, but I don't know if we got anywhere. You know I never stopped loving Frank. But sometimes with all of this heartache it's causing, I wish I'd never come back to Asheville. Then, it's sad that the only time I feel at peace is when I'm in his arms."

"True love is like that, Baby," Mae Mae said, with moisture filling her eyes. "That kinda love don't come but every so often in dis life. I sho' loved yo' Daddy, Jacob like dat. An' he loved me da same way.

"I neva tol' you much about Jacob. Seem like him an' me had such a short time ta getha. But, Lord! How I loved dat man. How we loved each otha."

"Yep. I wish I could have known him, Mama. I really do."

"Well, you look in da mirror an' you'll see him. Look like that Injun just spit you right out. Baby, he was such as good man. Back when I was a young woman, forced to be wit' dat evil man Red, Jacob was my angel. Like God sent him ta let me know dat life won't all bad an' evil.

"He was kinda wild. An' jus' liked to be out in nature in dem' woods, jus' stayin' alive how eva' he could. He talked 'bout his Mama an' family sometime livin' on dat reservation. But he refused to be cooped up like dat. He wanted ta run free and jus' be a real man, in his own little worl'.

"Nobody could tell him what ta do or where ta go, or where he had to live. I jus' loved dat about him. Jacob was totally free in every way."

Esther just closed her eyes and imagined this beautiful human being whose blood flowed in her veins. She thought of how proud she was of him even though she would never have the opportunity to know him. She hungered to know more and more.

"We called our meetin' place 'paradise.' It was me an' Jacob's secret place. But fa me it was my moment to git away for a while from my hell with Red. We'd meet an' talk an' laugh like won't nobody else in the whole wide worl'.

"An talkin' 'bout handsome! Jacob was a beautiful man from head ta toe. He was tall with skin 'bout the same color o' yours. His hair was down his back and it was dark as night and soft as fine fur.

"Those muscles of his was bustin' out everywhere. But when he held me or touched me, it was tender as a small chile. His dark brown eyes looked deep inside and talked to my heart without eva speakin' a word. Yep. He was a good man inside an' out.

"Even though Red beat and raped me many a day, I neva knew da love of two human beings could be like what me and Jacob had. Nope not 'til Jacob, my angel came into my life.

"But then God took Jacob away an' gave you to me. My prayer was answered, when I saw right off dat you was really Jacob's chile, an' not Red's. Wasn't no mistakin' dat, Chile. An' God only knows how much Jacob would've loved you if he could've."

"Thank you Mama," Esther said, in a sad low voice. "Thank you for sharing that stuff I never knew. We both have been through a lot. But we both for sure have really loved and been loved."

Mae Mae sniffed loudly, wiped her nose with the back of her hand and hugged Esther like she never had before.

"Dis fam'ly of ours been through some thangs. And we had some messed up times. We been trying to learn how ta' love our whole lives. Sometimes I've missed it. Sometimes I don't git it. But I ain't neva' gone give up. So, promise me you won't eitha, Baby. Family is so important in dis' worl'"

"But! Back to you and Frank. It's gone be alright, Baby. But you need ta pray. You need ta know God, Esther. I can't neva git you to see dat. With stuff like dis' where people hurtin', God got da only answer."

CHAPTER THIRTEEN

Donnell Crawford looked over to his right and two pews back at Pipe Daddy with a look of irritation. In the midst of all of the quiet, Pipe Daddy coughed deeply and loudly bringing up mucus that no one cared to imagine its current location. Though everyone else was aware of the infraction, only Donnell glanced over as if to sternly bring control.

The dark, heavy set man, dressed neatly in a gray suit and black tie, imagined himself as one who "knew how to act." He had never been inside of St. Lawrence before today. But even in this strange worship environment, "they could at least act right. Folks like Pipe Daddy didn't have no business coming here anyway," he thought.

Educated at North Carolina Central University in Durham, Donnell Crawford was one of the fortunate few who had had the opportunity to go to college in the fifties. He finished with a Bachelors in business, but then dropped out after a year in the School of Law, and returned home to Asheville and Eastend. From there, he went on to be a successful insurance agent.

Life insurance was beginning to be a must for hard working Negroes. Those who really cared for their loved ones had two goals when obtaining insurance. First of all, no one wanted to leave a bunch of bills behind and secondly the financial burden of a funeral should never be left behind for others. Plus it was always nice to leave a little spending change, if possible.

But since more and more people where buying the famous 'fiftycent policies,' business men like Donnell were doing pretty well for themselves.

And Mae Mae was his best customer. She knew well the benefits of life insurance, having been the beneficiary of Ma Letty's policy years ago. She was an easy sell, because that policy of Ma Letty's literally bought and paid for her Eastend Café.

Mae Mae was not only sold on the need for life insurance, she was the best promoter that Donnell could have. When she spread the word he got more and more customers. He simply loved Mae Mae for boosting his business and his career.

Donnell would not have missed being present this day, at the St. Lawrence Cathedral to support her in her time of loss. It was the least he could do.

Frank and Esther had not met at *The Sky Club* for at least two weeks. It had been a time away that they both needed, but did not really want. There was a lot to think about. There was a lot to talk about. There was a lot to do.

"Hello Baby," Frank said, finding Esther already there and at their special table.

"Hi," she stood, kissed him and whispered in his ear. "I missed you."

Frank just sat down beside her at the table and held her hand. For at least a moment, spoken language was not necessary. Communication was in their eyes and in their touch.

"It's been a while, huh?" Frank said, breaking the silence. "But a lot has happened since I saw you last. Could you feel the world spinning around?" he said laughing, showing those beautiful white teeth.

"Oh, like what? What happened?"

He took a deep breath, released it then looked her straight in the eye. "I told her," he said, as if no other words were needed.

Both of them were quiet again, but in a different way than before. This time they sat silently, looking down at the table, feeling a sense of doom even in the midst of pure love.

"What did she say?" Esther asked, almost in a whisper. "Is she OK?"

"Well, let me put it this way. She was not happy. She basically cussed me out and told me not to even think about getting a divorce or taking my son."

"I see. And you said?"

"But the clincher was, Mildred was willing to let me continue being with you with certain conditions. She insisted that she and I must still live the life of a couple. You know, she wanted to maintain the great fantasy of husband, wife, child, dog and white picket fence."

"My God, Frank! How could any of us live like that? Why in the world would she even want to?"

"All I know is Mildred really wants to maintain the lifestyle she and I always had. She also knows there's no way in hell I'm giving up my son. She would hold that over my head like you would not believe."

"Well that answers our question," Esther said, looking down with disappointment written on her face. "That's it in a nut shell. Both of us know you'll never leave your son, even for our true love."

"Oh Esther, my beautiful Esther, oh how I love you. These feelings I have right now are pulling me apart. I simply adore both you and my son. I am forced to decide between the one and only woman in the world for me and my son, who I need to raise like a man should.

"The thing is, Mildred knew she had won when she bargained with my child. She planned to use him for insurance for herself way back when Jack was conceived."

"It's so much for us to think about, Frank," she said, with tears welling in her eyes. "I know you love Jack as much as I love Jacob. I can't hold that against you. I'd be just as torn as you if I had to make a decision. I don't know, my Darling. I just don't know," she said, taking his hand and finding his soul through his eyes.

Once their eyes connected and they traveled together to their souls, again they didn't need words. They simply rose hand in hand and walked to the room that had become their 'paradise'

Neither of them knew when or how they undressed. They just found themselves in the heat of their touching bodies entwined together as if one.

The actual joining of their bodies was not sexual. It was fulfilling a drastic need to join one human being with another, with no space between them. It was breathing in unison, moaning in unison, just being.

Esther always knew the queenly role Frank allowed her to enjoy. So without hesitation, she climbed on top and mounted him. She leaned over in the midst of her slow rhythmic movement and whispered in his ear. "You are the love of my life."

This gesture caused Frank to stop momentarily as his movement that had been in perfect unison to hers, suddenly seized. In that moment, in that time, he just looked at her. Then once his eyes took in the beauty, the sensuality, the power moving above him, he pulled her forward wanting to be as close as possible.

This was not simple love making. It was mutual giving of one person to another in every way possible. As they touched, every part of their bodies, rediscovered over and over and over again that only God could have intended this union.

Kisses served as a way to bond and share something, anything. And Frank's penetration and thrusts, though just forceful enough, provided exactly what both of them needed. The extraordinary need to feel and nothing else was satisfied at the ultimate level.

When they climaxed it was more like an explosion. It was like an eruption of a volcano spewing lava all over the world. It was a feeling so momentous that they wanted to hold on forever. But reality kicked in as swiftly as his erection was gone and she rolled to her side.

Exhausted, both rolled to their backs. And just a glance at Esther showed tears rolling down the sides of her face and onto the pillow. It was a quiet cry. It was not a loud verbal, sniffling cry.

There were just quiet tears and the beating of her heart.

"Oh! Baby! Please don't do that," Frank said, as he glanced over and noticed her tears.

"I can't help it!" Esther said, sitting up reaching for a tissue near the bed. "I just know what I need to do that's all. And, it's not easy."

"What Baby? What are you thinking?"

"This is the last time I can do this, Frank. I can't live like this. I can't be your mistress behind closed doors. And I refuse to come between you and Jack. I just won't do it."

"So, this is it? Is that what you're sayin'?"

"This is it. And please, my Darling, make it easy on both of us. No goodbyes. Just dress and leave and I'll leave a while later. I'll see you around and after a while we'll be the best of friends again. It's just gonna take some time."

"I understand. But do something for me too. Please, never, ever forget, how much I love you."

CHAPTER FOURTEEN

Flossie and her daughter Ida sat among the other Eastend crowd looking totally lost, but comfortable to be so close to others they were acquainted with. Ida just happened to be home from Bennett College and she nor Flossie would have missed being here.

Flossie had raised five children as a single mother in the Lee Walker Heights 'projects.' Five children were difficult anywhere, but especially for a single, Negro woman and especially in Lee Walker Heights, also known as Diaper Hill.

Ida was Flossie's youngest and the one she considered her last hope for "makin' it." All three of the boys were in jail, Loretta the other girl, was raising her own two year old and Ida was a freshman at Bennett College in Greensboro.

Flossie had an eighth grade education and worked in Biltmore Forest as a domestic. But Lord knows, she always wanted the best for her kids. And Ida was fulfilling that dream, by being the first in the family to attend college.

They glanced at Mae Mae in the front pew of the church, feeling for her as she cried quietly. It was almost like she was holding back her grief so that she would not disturb anything in the unusually quiet church. But they could tell by her eyes how sad and hurt she was. And it hurt them and most of the others around them, that she was so sad.

Flossie remembered fondly back two years ago when Ida was invited to be in the Zeta's Debutante Ball. She didn't even know what a doggone Zeta or Debutante Ball was back then. But the sponsor who was a member of the Zeta Phi Beta Sorority said it could be the chance for Ida to get a scholarship to go to college. That's all Flossie needed to hear. She would do everything in her power to make it happen.

These Balls began as upper-crust events that copied rich Whites who introduced high school age girls 'properly' into society. In most cases the parents of the Negro girls who were invited had money. They were the daughters of teachers, lawyers, doctors, etc. But in some cases girls with smarts, ambition and potential from poorer families might be invited. This was the case with Ida.

Neither Ida nor Flossie had any idea about the work or anything else that was involved. Most Debutantes donated money to the Sorority, bought a long, white formal dress and heels and found an escort for the evening. And because Ida had no money, no white dress, no nothing, it seemed like, no way.

Flossie smiled to herself looking over at Mae Mae again. "That Lady somethin' else," she thought. "If it won't for Mizz Mae, my Baby wouldn't have got the money she needed for that Ball. An' she wouldn't have been dancin' around that ballroom flo' wit' dem otha' girls like she did.

"Mizz Mae donated money an' bought Ida's outfit right outta her own pocket. If it wasn't for her, no tellin' where Ida'd be right now. Yep! We love that lady."

It was Sunday morning, and like clockwork Mae Mae and Little Jacob were preparing for church. Mae Mae started the morning by pouring cereal and milk in a bowl and combing Jacob's hair while he ate. It was war on both counts.

Jacob never liked to eat, and every stroke of the comb took way too much effort, as Mae Mae pulled through his thick, naturally curly hair. With each and every stroke she was met with opposition and whining.

"Gran'ma! dat hurt!" Jacob said, as he turned his head toward the strokes in hopes of minimizing the pain. "Ouch!"

"Jus' turn aroun' an' eat yo breakfast!" Mae Mae shouted. "I ain't got time, dis mornin'. I really ain't got time. You hear. Eat yo' cereal and let me do dis nappy stuff. I wish to hell you got hair from your Mama and not my side o' da fam'ly."

"Mama! Mama! Don't start that cussing" Esther said, entering the kitchen, already dressed for church. "I'm going with ya'll this morning."

"Oh my God in heaven! Mae Mae said. "What in God's name makin' you go to church finally? It's gone sho' rain today," she said, laughing.

"I just finally want to go back and give God a chance," she said. "Anyway, I never really left God. I just left the church."

"Well, it's a blessin' no matter where it's comin' from. Thanks be to God!"

They entered St. James AME Zion Church as Mae Mae led and Esther and Jacob followed. Mae Mae went directly to the pew that she had claimed for years as her own. There was never a debate about it for her or the other members who had "paid their dues." They had earned those seats with age and wisdom.

Heads were turning as they entered. Most knew the celebrity status of Esther and the fact that she was Mae Mae's daughter. This would of course call attention anyway. But they had never seen Esther at St. James since she returned to Asheville. This created an air of curiosity as well as excitement. But in no time at all, the real show began.

The women's choir marched in from the back. They were robed in burgundy choir robes with high heels that posed as the only way to show each woman's own unique style. They marched with sophistication and distinction, together yet individually. They took their time, step by step in harmony with the organ.

Once the choir was in place, Pastor Goins took his seat, as if on a throne. They rocked him into his seat with a loud rhythmic song and clapping. These gestures were said to be praise and worship, but they served as his own special introduction to the platform.

The choir director motioned directions to the choir by eyes, hands and body gestures that became a performance of its own. And in response, the choir gave it all they had, even before the actual service had begun.

The sounds and the excitement derived just from the song was enough to move the congregation to the heights of praise necessary for the sermon to begin. Everyone knew the song only served as the great precursor to the Word. Everyone knew this was only the beginning.

Pastor Goins stood and raised both hands, exercising the only true control in the whole room. He raised his hands with a purpose. He raised his hands to show that once again, he and he only had the authority to interpret God's true Word in this particular place, this very morning.

"Good Mornin' children of God!" he said loudly. "Thanks be to God!"

The congregation shifted like clockwork from the loud exuberant praises brought by thumping music, to the smooth cool praise that came so naturally to Pastor Goins. Most were already on their feet before he even completed a full sentence.

"We got a lot to talk about this mornin'," he said. "Can I git a Amen?

"Ya'll know some time we got thangs we jus' don't won't ta talk about. You know. We got some families try to put on blinders an' pretend they don't see what's goin' on. But God tol' me, Church, we got to talk about this today.

"I don't know why, and I don't neva question my God, but I'm gone jus' talk plain. We got some thangs that we try to look ova' like they ain't there. But ain't no getting' around our Father. 'Cause I tell ya'll each an' every Sunday. God knows all!

"I want you to turn in your Bible to Exodus 20. Let me just say, Church, that Exodus 20 is not playin'. Amen? I have to say even for myself, that if you can abide by all the rules in this Chapter, you tryin' for Sainthood." Everyone laughed, as they held on to the thought.

"Most of Exodus 20 says, Thou shall not this and thou shall not that. But one of the first things it says that jumps right out at me is, "*I am the Lord thou God which have brought you out of the land of Egypt. Thou shalt not have other gods before me.*"

"I hear ya'll sayin' 'Oh! I got this. I know it ain't but one God. I ain't tryin' to honor no other gods.'

"But keep this in mind. The Bible ain't actually talkin' about you just honorin' other gods. Remember when you puttin' other people and food, and money, and houses and all that stuff first, it's the same thang as havin' other gods before the true Almighty God. Ya'll hear what I'm sayin' to you?

"And when I look at Exodus 20:17, my God, Children! Well, all I'm gonna say is listen and see where you fit. And If you say you doin' good on all counts, call me for an individual counseling session as soon as possible," he said, hopping around with a chuckle.

"Listen closely, Saints. *'Thou shalt not covet thy neighbor's house, thou shalt not covet thy neighbor's wife, nor his manservant, nor his maidservant, nor his ox, nor his ass, nor any thing that is thy neighbor's.'*

"Now! Let's just close our eyes an' let that sink in for a minute," he said, suddenly sitting still and quiet.

Mae Mae, Esther and Jacob were all following closely, but for different reasons. Mae

Mae was thinking about the full verse and pondering if she indeed had at least tried to follow most things on the list. Jacob was enjoying the Pastor's demand to sit still and quiet, as if he was playing 'Simon Says.'

And Esther just waited. Somehow she knew this message was meant just for her. She knew as much as she had tried to avoid a real relationship with God, that was who brought her here this day, this time, this sermon. She took a deep breath and prepared for what was to come.

"OK, Church!" Pastor Goins said, finally breaking the silence. "Now we all know we ain't got no problem with the ox and the ass in Exodus. Amen?" he said, with a loud laugh. "I can't even say that we got problems with manservants or maidservants. But! Church! Thy neighbor's house and thy neighbor's wife? Well? Come on now.

"Let me put it this way, Church. Ya'll gone think I'm crazy. An' believe me, I ain't judgin.' But I go to *Mae Mae's Eastend Café* sometime on Friday nights. You know, 'cause I just have to have some of that fried fish."

Everybody laughed and turned to Mae Mae. She looked down with a slight blush, knowing exactly where he was going.

"So we all from Eastend, so we know mo' goes on in that Café than just eatin'. Amen? There's some dark corners up in there where slow dancin' goes to a whole 'nother level," he said, with his head way back, laughing deeply.

"An' sometimes, the wife or the husband got left at the house. Amen?

"Anyway, I know Miss Mae wantin' me to get off that real quick," he said, looking her way with a smile. "An' like I said, I ain't here to judge. I just want ya'll to know that coveting anything that wasn't given to you, 'specially by the Lord thy God, is a sin.

"You can just think of stuff too, folks. Your desires that you just think about can get you in trouble. That's the bad thing. You can be all good and proper and thinkin' you the most spiritual thang that ever lived. But if you thinkin' about Miss So an' So or Mr. So and So after a good ole slow drag at the Café. You better check yo'self.

"It's sad sometime, Church. God intends for us to be with that one special person he chooses for us in life. And Lord knows sometime that just don't work out. You know. You men be going crazy. You wanna 'have yo' cake an' eat it too'. Anybody know what I'm sayin' here today?" he said, jumping around, knowing he was connecting.

"An' I ain't gonna just blame it on the men. You ladies know sometime, somewhere in the late of night it gets too good to let go. An' I ain't talkin' about with yo' husband."

Esther looked down, and twisted in her seat. She could feel little beads of sweat forming on her forehead. Everything was involuntary. Now Esther, the most expert manipulator of emotions through her singing, was having a hard time.

"But Church! The good news is that God still loves us. God loves us no matter what. And God knew that after the sins of Adam and Eve, we would all be born sinners. So he just expects us to know it, believe in him and ask for forgiveness.

"That is why God sent his son, Jesus Christ, to suffer and die to save us. Yes Church, if we believe and have undying faith then we are saved! We are saved! We are indeed saved."

Pastor Goins finished and stepped away from the microphone as if there was no questions or debate about what he just shared. He took his seat and waited for the song where he would do 'the ask.' He knew there were souls in the church today that needed to be saved. His job was only to ask.

After moments of contemplation, he rose with the appearance of much less drama than any other time in the service. His words were quietly delivered, yet very sincere.

"It's that time in the service, Church, where I am led by Jesus Christ to ask anyone present if they want to accept Jesus as their very own Lord and Savior. You must only do this once in your life. Why not come today? Why not accept Jesus and change your life forever, today?"

Mae Mae looked over at Esther with tears in her eyes and hope in her heart, but Esther didn't move.

CHAPTER FIFTEEN

Everyone in the church seemed to be idle and waiting for something, anything to happen. The priest now faced away from them and towards the casket and the big cross in the front and center. He performed certain movements with his hands in addition to speaking Latin and bowing his head.

By now, Little Jacob was restless and getting stern looks from the adults surrounding him on both sides. His heart felt sad because they said it should when people died. But he didn't understand where dead people go. He didn't believe you couldn't ever see them again. So if he had it his way, everything would be back to normal after they finished looking at that man up there talking funny.

He'd been having a good time lately with his Mama and that nice man named Frank and his little boy named Jack too.

"But sometime I don't like Jack," Jacob thought to himself as he tried his best to understand that man up in the front of the church. "Jack always want to see Superman on TV. He didn't never wanna see nothin' else. Well, 'Lassie' an' 'Dennis the Menace' my fav'rite.

"My Gran'mama got us a TV, an' before I go to bed, I get to see what I want to. I don't like 'Superman' though.

"'Dennis the Menace' is real bad! But he don't neva git no spankin's. Mr. Wilson act like he didn't like him. But Dennis still like him though. Oh yeah and I tol' my Mama I want a dog jus' like 'Lassie'. I want my dog to help people too. Mama

*said she was gonna get me a 'Lassie' when I git big.
I can't wait.*

*"Oh! Oh! Oh! Mickey Mouse! Yeah he my
fav'rite too. I be watchin' them children dance an'
sing wit' them big Mickey ears on dey head.*

*"I wanna watch TV all the time. My Mama
gonna let me too.*

*"Gran'mama teached me my prayers at
night. She say, 'Now I lay me down to sleep. I pray
the Lord my soul to keep. If I should die before I
wake, I pray to da Lord my soul to take'. Maybe dat
man up dere 'spose to say dat."*

*Jacob felt a tug at his arm and knew
instantly it was a silent demand to pay attention. He
complied as he looked up at the White man in the
dress up front.*

*So, he would turn around now and try to
listen. But he couldn't wait until they got back in
that big black car and he could go home and see
'The Flintstones' tonight.*

Frank was seldom at home but this was
Sunday evening and he needed to take this
opportunity to talk to Mildred. His head was still
spinning from the break up with Esther about a
month ago. But he had not been able to talk about it
to anyone, especially with Mildred, until now. He
was finally beginning to come down out of the
clouds to face a broken heart, for the second time in
his life.

Taking advantage of this time at home, he
went into Jack's room before anything else. Noise
and talking came from the room as if Jack had

company. He looked up noticing Frank's entry and ran to him and jumped up into his arms.

Jack was dressed in a small fireman's helmet and had been making the sound of a siren while he pushed a toy fire engine around the room. But the pure joy of being in his father's arms made him completely happy.

"Daddy! Daddy!" he said, still in Frank's arms. "Come an' play. Please?"

"I'll play for a minute, OK? Then I have to go back and chat with Mommy. Have you been good today?"

"Yes, Daddy. Mommy let me watch TV. I saw Caspa da Ghos', Little LuLu, an' Pop Eye Sailor Man. I love TV Daddy."

"I know you do, son. Oh! Remember we're 'sposed to go to Westgate and ride those fun rides out there. Right?"

"Yeah, Daddy. But I ain't gonna ride dat big ole ferrous wheel. I'm scared, Daddy."

Frank laughed loudly as he looked at his son who was younger and smaller, but otherwise an exact replica of him. Love showed in his eyes, in his touch, in his voice.

"OK! Who are we saving from the fire? Turn the siren on so we can get there in time. We don't want anybody to get hurt, do we?"

"No, Daddy."

They played until Jack and Frank were exhausted. Frank bathed him, put him to bed and headed down the stairs.

As Frank descended the stairs, he could already feel the tension in the air. He and Mildred had not really had much to say since the stand down at the restaurant. Neither of them was looking forward to this conversation.

"Mildred! We need to talk," Frank said.

"Well, well, well," she replied. "I've been waitin' for this moment. I thought it wasn't never gonna come."

"I guess the first thing you should know is that I talked to Esther. She basically decided she didn't want to have anything to do with me if you refused to give me a divorce."

"I don't blame a Sista," Mildred said, almost gleefully.

"I know none of this means a damn thing to you," Frank shouted. "You just want what you want. But just know this, Mildred. Keeping me here will never make me love you. Just know, I will never love anyone like I love Esther. Do you understand?"

"Oh yes. I completely understand. I know I ain't neva had you, Frank. I jus' settled knowing if I looked good and gave you good pussy when you wanted it, everything would be OK. Then her ass had to come back."

"And don't think you pulled anything over on me. I know you got pregnant with Jack just for insurance. You never wanted children at first. You were too vain. But, you know, I've got to give it to you. That detail alone changed the whole doggone game."

"Frank, we got businesses. We got a fantastic home. We got a beautiful kid. I'm just not ready to give all that up. Not for dat Bitch anyway. I paid my dues, Sweetheart."

By now, Frank was steaming mad. Being a numbers man, he hated to be beat with such finality. Once again, the love of his life was lost.

As they both attempted to calm down, knowing stalemate when they saw it, the phone rang. Mildred went to the table to answer. She knew that Frank was never there enough to answer the phone anyway.

"Hello?" she said, slightly irritated, wondering who in the world would be calling at such an hour.

Hello," a familiar voice responded. "May I please speak to Frank?"

"Who is this?" Mildred said, knowing, but not really wanting to know.

"This is Esther, Mildred. I hate to disturb your home. But I hope you will let me speak to Frank. It's sort of an emergency."

"Well, I'm sure you know the arrangement I was willing to go with. So I ain't gone keep you from talkin' to him. He ain't goin' nowhere. We both know dat. Hol' on."

Mildred turned to Frank like a hurricane coming through. She called him over and threw the phone at him, as she walked away. "Dat's yo Bitch on the line," she said. "I guess she goin' wit' my terms."

"Hello!" Frank said, with an adrenaline rush like never before. "What's wrong? You OK? You never call here. But I'm so glad to hear your voice, I don't know what to do."

"Frank, listen to me. I am dealing with something right now that I had to talk to you about. I simply cannot handle this alone. Even if I said we are through, we have to talk about this."

"What wrong, Honey? Just tell me what wrong."

"Frank, I'm pregnant."

Silence kicked in partly because this was the only person on earth he would ever want to have a baby with, and partly because he was shocked beyond belief that Esther was even on the other end of the phone. This was a real shock.

"My God! Esther. We really do need to meet and discuss this. I'll be in touch soon, I promise."

"What…what was that click on the other line?" she said.

"I don't know. It's OK. I'll be in touch soon."

Within a few moments, Mildred appeared back in the room with a strange look on her face. Frank was too much in shock to even notice.

"Well, what did yo' woman want?" Mildred said. "Sound like she kinda desperate or somethin'."

"Mildred, just do me a favor. I'm doing things the way you wanted, OK? I just need a little space right now. OK?"

"Yep, you got it," she said. I'm cool. I'm cool. Believe me, I'm cool."

The night ended just as it always did the past few months. Mildred retired to what used to be their bedroom, alone. Frank sat up deeply in thought before falling into a deep sleep in one of the other bedrooms.

125

Frank's dream this night was a happy dream. He dreamed he was living happily ever after with the love of his life, his son Jack, Jacob and their new baby. He dreamed of a loving peaceful home filled with hugs and kisses and joy.

He saw everything he always longed for, yet felt somehow, he somehow would never have. Then he fell into a deep sleep.

CHAPTER SIXTEEN

Pastor Goins was in attendance at the Funeral Mass along with the other Eastend crowd. Mae Mae was a long time church member and generous donor to St. James, so now it was time to be there for her.

Like most of the other folks, the Pastor had never had a reason to visit the St. Lawrence Cathedral. But he was quite intrigued with the way 'those Catholics did things.' "This was certainly not the way I would do a home going," he thought to himself. "But who am I to think one way or the other? Nobody even asked my advice."

He knew these Eastend folks very well, and he could look around at them and tell, they were bored as hell. His folks needed some good ole loud Gospel music and some preachin' that'll send that chile off right.

"That priest up there already did the part of the service that's in English, where he was talkin' about the deceased. But Lord knows I didn't get nothin' out of it. Nobody else did either. 'Cause when he finished everybody was lookin' around like, 'that's all'. Soon after that it was Latin only. An' can't none of us understand that.

"I just think we all got one way to come into this world. And we got one way to leave this world. And everybody deserve the best sendoff possible.

"You got to 'make a joyful noise' as they say. You got to sing, and shout, and dance, and cry, and laugh. I know the deceased don't know one way or the other. But maybe it's just for the family. It's just a way to show how much people care.

"I done a many a funeral at St. James and none of 'em ever been this quiet. But anyway, we here for our sista, Mae Mae."

Esther was simply lost as she sat quietly in the darkness of her booth in the back of the Café, She was glad this was not her night to perform. There was no way tonight that she could give a part of herself to an audience, she thought. With all of the things twirling around in her head, there was nothing else to give.

The music on the jukebox was slow and mellow. This was just what she needed right now. She needed just to mellow out and go deep inside herself. She needed to begin to accept her sadness, her grief, her loss. But she also needed to remember the things she should be thankful for.

Marvin Gaye was crooning, *'What's Goin' On,'* as she leaned her head way back and closed her eyes. When she opened her eyes and glanced down she saw the carving on the table from long ago. F J loves E R was carved deeply into the table as if it would be there forever. She traced it with her finger as tears rolled down her cheeks.

The aromas of her favorites were coming from the kitchen. The fried chicken, fried okra, fried green tomatoes and collards passed by her table several times, as she looked up at Bessie's toothless smile. But tonight, even her favorites could not force her to have an appetite. She had not been able to enjoy food this entire full month of pregnancy.

"OK, now I know somethin' wrong when you passin' up fried okra," Mae Mae said, sitting opposite Esther in the booth. "What's up wit' you young lady?"

Esther bowed her head hoping Mae Mae would not see her tears. She wiped with the back of her hand, and attempted to smile.

"I'm OK, Mama. I just got a lot on my mind that's all."

"Well, you wanna talk? You know I love you! And you know I'm always here fa you, no matter what. Right?"

"Yes, I do know that, Mama," Esther said, sniffing with her runny nose. "I don't never doubt that anymore, Mama. If there's one thing I found out since I moved back to Asheville, you are a good and carin' woman, and everybody really loves you."

"Yep, I got a lot o' children roun' here, don't I?" she said, laughing her laugh. "I was jus' thinkin' the otha' day 'bout how far dis family done come. Lord knows I started takin' care of my Mama, Cora Lee's babies she ain't neva wanted. I got sol' off to dat mean ass, evil Red an' had to run fa my life.

"Ain't nontin' but by da grace o' God, dat I met Looney on dat road dat day. Den' Looney brung me to my angel, Ma Letty. An' Baby my story go on an' on to havin' you an' Elijah. To findin' forgiveness. To getting' the Café. To you comin' back as a star.

"Lordy! Lordy! Can you see it my Da'lin' chile? Can you see dat God been done had a plan fa me from da very minute I was born. He got a plan fo' us all. We jus' gotta have faith an' rare back and go for da ride dat he got for us. Ain't but one plan, an' dat's His!

"My las' prayer on dis here earth is dat you fin' dat faith, dat peace, dat plan in yo' life. I want my beautiful baby girl to know God."

And they sat in a loud silence in the Café, in deep thought. They looked out of the double doors as people entered and heard a hard rain pattering down on the pavement. Someone just happened to play a song on the jukebox that they were both needed to hear right at that time.

Strange Kind o' Love. Every love just ain't the same. Some is good and some is strange. Some I give and some I make. Some ain't worth the time it takes. It's a strange kin o' love. Some will last and some will end. Some just beggin' to begin. It's strange, so strange. ...And the Strangest Love is mine.

They cried for the same things and for different things, as they sat there together. It seemed all of their senses were kicking in all at once. The smells of the food, the noise of the crowd, the pitter patter of the rain, the warm glow of the Café and just the love, overwhelmed them both.

CHAPTER SEVENTEEN

Sheila Flynn looked at Mae Mae and the family in the front pew of the church. She knew that nobody could do Esther's hair like she could. Esther had gained confidence in her abilities over time and she was the only one she trusted.

It's well known that Black women don't entrust just any beautician with their hair. But Sheila was one of the best in Asheville and she knew it. For hair as beautiful as Esther's, one always in front of the public, she had to be good.

Sheila noticed when she looked at Esther after doing her hair for the funeral, that she'd done it perfectly once again. The soft, jet black hair, shampooed and cut just below her shoulders with a slight wave in the bangs, was looking good. "It always did," she thought.

She remembered that conversations were always lively when the two of them got together. Neither one of them ever held back. Sheila was a heavyset, short, dark skinned, very talkative woman. She was known for her outspokenness and her ability to 'tell it like it is.' And these were the qualities that Esther loved best about her.

"What's goin' on with you and Frank Jordan, Girl?" she asked, while combing out Esther's hair. Girl, you know how these folks in Asheville talk! Don't nothin' git by these people." She laughed that laugh that sounded like a sneaky child.

"Well you know you just like a sister to me, Esther. I'll whoop somebody's ass if they talk too bad about you. You jus' do yo' thang, my Sister.

True love is too hard to find. So you love that man if you want to. You hear me! Don't pay no mind to these jealous people, Girl.

"You remember Steve James? Well he was so damn fine. Girl, I just couldn't help myself. In fact, I got into him down at yo' Mama's place.

He was as married as can be, but he came over and asked me to slow dance. And that was all it took. I been seeing him on the side ever since. An' you know what? It's just like that song, 'Ain't Nobody's Business if I Do.' We all deserve to be happy in this life.

"See you again soon. I love you, Girl! You are truly a special person," she said, as she left the room.

Esther was still waiting to hear from Frank after the telephone call to his home. She knew she was taking a big chance calling there with the possibility of Mildred answering.

But the news of her pregnancy hit her so hard that she needed desperately to talk to him. At this point she was two months along, and some decisions needed to be made before she began to show.

Finally Frank called her at the Café and Mae Mae showed a look of motherly concern, as she handed Esther the phone.

"Hey Baby," he said. "I know you thought I would never get back to you, but I've been torn up by all this. I know you have been too."

"Oh Frank. You just don't know. I just don't know what to do. But I can't talk here."

"I know, Baby. I won't you to take a ride with me. OK? Can you take a drive with me and be away all day tomorrow?"

"Yes, I'll make arrangements."

"OK, I'll pick you up at about ten in the morning. Come to the McCormick Baseball field and we'll leave your car there."

It seemed like the night would never end and sleep would never come after she tucked Jacob in to bed. Esther paced for a while then took a long bath and settled in to her bed. When her alarm sounded and daylight shined through her window, somehow she felt better.

She arrived at the baseball field parking lot at a little bit before ten. Frank was already there sitting, anxiously waiting. They had not actually seen each other since the last time they met at the *Skyland Club*. And though the plan at that time was that they would not be lovers ever again, the love in their eyes still showed.

"Hello Esther," Frank said, as he got out of his car and helped her into to the passenger side. "You just don't know how happy I am to see you."

"Hi, Frank," she said, seating herself in the seat, as he closed her door. "I should have known it would be more complicated than just saying goodbye and walking out of your life."

Frank laughed as he drove off on an adventure that should have been a delightful time. But the stress that both of them felt this day was not what either one looked forward to.

"So where are we going?" she asked.

"I want to take you to a special place, where we can get away for a while. I mean really get away!

"We're going down the mountain to Cherokee. The drive will be beautiful. The scenery will be just what we need, and just maybe being that close to God will clear or minds."

"That sounds good," she said, closing her eyes.

They drove the winding roads leading to Cherokee. The remarkable beauty of the multi-colored trees providing a portrait of the mountains, was like a gift from God. It was breathtaking. It was like they were living God's plan. Like they must travel this particular road, on this day and on this very path, to see it.

"This view is simply beautiful," she said. "What made you think of this?"

"I just knew we needed to get away. We needed to get away as far as possible."

"It's perfect. I really needed this, Frank."

They pulled over at an overlook on the side of the road and Frank parked. He opened her door and they both went toward the brick barrier and stood in awe. They were looking at the most beautiful sight they had ever seen.

The recently fallen leaves, still beautiful, now spoke to them through senses they didn't know they had. For what felt like hours, yet were only moments, they looked out over what seemed to be miles and miles of a portrait painted just for them. And they held on tightly in an embrace that both of them needed desperately.

"I love you," Frank said, looking into her eyes. "I hate myself for ever thinking I could let you just walk out of my life again."

"Frank, just tell me what you think we can do. I certainly cannot be in Asheville, in Eastend with a baby on the way and no husband. That just won't work."

"I know," he said. "I know now, that I want to, I must be with you. We may have to go away and relocate. I don't know. But I'm not going to let you get away again."

"What about Mildred? And I know you're not leaving Jack. We already talked about that."

"I'm getting a divorce. And I will have my son," he said, with determination in his voice. "I want to be your husband. I want us to raise our child, our children, together."

"Let's go now. I know the perfect place in Cherokee that I want you to see."

They climbed back into the car and continued down the winding road. Once they reached the bottom, suddenly out of nowhere, Indian souvenir shops and the Indian village appeared. The natives in costumes and the very atmosphere of the Cherokee Nation made them smile.

"So what is this special place? " Esther asked.

"Just wait and see, young lady."

They drove further and past the main strip to some of the back roads. And after a while they arrived and Frank pulled over and parked. Again, he opened her door and helped her out.

"This is Our Lady of Guadalupe Church," Frank said. "I drove by here once before and thought it was so beautiful. It sits here on the side of this mountain so peaceful. I've never seen anything like it ever before."

"Oh my God!" Esther shouted, with emotions that came from nowhere. "Can we go in?"

"Yep. I think they leave it open for tourists. People just go in pray and leave a donation. So it pays to leave it open."

They walked cautiously down the uneven terrain and to the front door. When they entered, they were captivated by the beauty that created a spiritual feeling that Esther had never felt before.

The centered stained glass window portrayed Our Lady of Guadalupe. The many colors hit by the sun streaming in from over the mountains, was so perfect that they thought they had died and gone to heaven. The blues, the greens, the reds and all of the colors had them spellbound as they stood in the door.

Esther ran to the altar and knelt as she looked up at the huge masterpiece before her. Frank just watched her as she was in her own spiritual element. And then she prayed.

"Lord God! Forgive me for drifting away from you for so long. I had so much on my heart. I had things that happened to me as a child in the name of God.

"And I just couldn't find you. I couldn't feel you taking care of me. But now I know you were there all the time. I feel you here and now. I am so

thankful to be here. And I do, my Lord, here and now, accept you as my Lord and Savior."

Frank approached her at the altar and waited for his turn to speak. "Esther, I have always loved you. And I feel there is no better time than now. Please will you marry me? I promise to get a divorce and live with you happily ever after."

"I love you too, Frank. My Mama just talked to me about God's plan for each and every one of us. There is a reason we are here in this place today. I have given my life to God this day. And I give my heart to you. So yes, I would love to be your wife."

They held hands and prayed together before they departed. When they returned to the car, a bright orange sun was setting in the midst of the mountains. Nothing else could have been a better ending to their special day.

Frank drove along, winding back up the mountain around the sharp curves. They approached home with a renewed spirit, though they realized a lot of things needed to be done to insure that they would soon be together.

As they arrived and he parked at the baseball field beside her car, they had a determination that nothing could stop them. They kissed long and hard and they separated and departed.

CHAPTER EIGHTEEN

Mae Mae looked around and for the first time since the Mass began noticed the many faces in the crowd behind her. All of her longtime friends and acquaintances she saw almost daily in the Café were there. She could feel their support. She could feel their love.

When she turned back around to face the altar, she had to blink several times. She didn't know if she was going crazy or if she was in a dream.

Standing up near the priest and next to the casket with her hands on her hips, was Ma Letty. Ma Letty's face showed pure love and peace, just as Mae Mae remembered her. It was the face she longed to see, especially now, especially in her time of grief.

"You know everthang gone be alright, don't you?" she heard Ma Letty say. "Girl! I been really lookin' afta you since I went away to be with God," Ma Letty's laugh a laugh that was unmistakable. "You ain't had no idea, did ya?

"Well, dats what angels do. They the people dat love ya so much they hang out some just ta look after you. That ain't nothin' new anyhow.

"I was yo' angel when I was alive and Looney delivered you on my doorstep. I fell in love wit' you right then an' there. You was so young an' you was hurtin' so bad.

I could tell life had treated you awful. An' I was determined if dere's anyway I could make it betta, I would.

"There was a lot o' bad thangs goin' on in dat family o' yours. An' I knew that's what made you question yo' love for your own son. But it wasn't nobody's fault but the devil hisself. Elijah was a evil child, but he finally came to know peace an' the Lord.

"So don't think I blame him for setting the fire that burned me up. Don't neva worry 'bout that. You hear me?

"I'm here to tell you, Baby. Don't worry 'bout yo' chile. God take care of us all when we leave dis worl' Jus' like when we livin'."

Mae Mae blinked again and Ma Letty was gone.

When she arrived home after the drive, Esther rushed into the house in search of Mae Mae. She rushed in almost out of breath with excitement.

"Mama! Mama!" she called out. "Where are you?"

Mae Mae ran out of Jacob's room thinking that something must be wrong. "I'm right here! What's the matter? You OK?"

"Mama, I couldn't wait to tell you all of the good news. And believe me. I got a lot of news to tell."

"What in the world happened, Esther?" Mae Mae asked, with her own excitement.

"Well, I wanted you to be the first to know. I finally made peace with my Father God! I asked God to forgive my sins and I accepted Him as my Lord and Savior!"

"What! When did all o' this happen, Girl?" Mae Mae said, jumping up and down and hugging her. "I'm so proud o' you, Baby! So, so proud!"

They went into the living room and sat together on the couch. This was a conversation Mae Mae had been praying about for a long time. She wanted to make sure she wasn't dreaming. And Esther wanted to tell her the whole story

"I went on a drive to Cherokee today with Frank. We had a lot to talk about, Mama. I haven't told another soul but Frank. I didn't know how to even tell you. But I'm pregnant, Mama. I'm having Frank's baby."

"Oh Lord! Esther."

"Well, that's what we talked about. Both of us had decided to break up until we knew about the baby. But now, he plans to divorce Mildred and marry me."

"This is just too much, Esther. Are ya'll sure 'bout this?

"No. But all we know is we've always been madly in love with each other and why shouldn't we finally be happy? He never loved Mildred, Mama. He never stopped loving me.

"But the most exciting news is my being saved, Mama. It was so wonderful. It was so unexpected, but so right. We went to this church in Cherokee and it was so beautiful sitting on the mountain; it was like being in heaven.

"I could feel God calling out to me time I came through the door of the church. And I looked at all of the bright colors from the sun shining just right through the beautiful stained glass window. It was the most peacefulness I had ever felt in my whole life. God was right there, Mama. He was there!"

"That sound so good, Baby. Every thang be in God's time. I jus' always had to keep tellin' myself dat."

"So, all in one day, I got saved, I accepted my pregnancy, and I got proposed to by the man I simply adore. I don't know how it's all gonna fit together, but I have faith that it will."

They sat together among the big pillows on the couch, letting it all sink in. The house was quiet now. But their minds and hearts were all over the place. One thing was certain. They needed God now more than ever.

The next day everything seemed so new. It was a brand new day for them all. Mae Mae was already gone to the Café when Esther and Jacob got up.

"Good morning my darling Jacob," Esther said. "How's my Baby boy today?"

"Fine." He said, short on words.

"I want to do something really special today. Just you and me," she said, cheerfully. What you think? Would you like that?"

"Yeah, I guess so."

"How's about we go to the Recreation Park Zoo? I always wanted to see all those wild animals. That sound good?"

"Oh yeah," Little Jacob said, more excited than before. "I love animals like I see in my books."

They drove out of Eastend and through the tunnel leading to Tunnel Road. The tunnel was dark, dusty and smoky. But as soon as they came to the end and saw daylight, it was another world.

The motels and stores and restaurants lined the street, each offering something better than the one before. It was a treat just driving down the unusually busy road.

When they arrived at the zoo, Jacob's face lit up with an excitement that Esther had not seen in a long time. They climbed out of the car and walked to the entrance. Esther bought the tickets and their adventure began.

"OK Baby, now don't get to close to the fence," Esther warned. "That leopard looks kinda hungry, huh?" as they both laughed.

They walked around to all of the cages and laughed, and talked as they saw the lion, the elephant, and the chimpanzee. When there was nothing more to see, they left the zoo and walked around the park before the trip home.

"That was so fun, Mommy!" Jacob said, going into the house. "I'm gonna always remember dat monkey. He was my favorite."

"I'm so glad we had fun today. Remember how much Mommy loves you, OK?"

CHAPTER NINETEEN

They filed out of the church quietly. Most were in thought remembering their own special times rather than this service that they couldn't understand. The black limos from Allen Funeral Home were lined up out front as the casket was placed in the first one.

Looking out of the window from the second car, Mae Mae noticed a strange man holding one hand up and holding a Bible in the other. The strange man was a homeless 'hippie' they called 'J Man.' He had blond shoulder length hair and dirty blue jeans with a large gray football jersey with the number eleven on the back.

They called him 'J Man' because he always appeared at the St. Lawrence Cathedral whenever there was a funeral. Somehow he knew that he needed to be there. When he wasn't at St. Lawrence, he could be seen just sitting quietly in Pack Square, holding his Bible.

But today he was here as they filed out to go to their cars. 'J Man' caught the eye of Mae Mae through the window of the limo once she was seated. She looked at him briefly and immediately noticed the kindness in his eyes. It was as if this was his purpose on earth. He was supposed to be here at this time, in this place to comfort her in her time of loss.

He opened his ragged Bible with missing pages as the Eastend crowd flowed from the church and headed for their cars. He began to read Psalm 103. The words were so perfect it seemed that time stood still. They all heard him no matter where they stood.

Psalm 103:1-5 -1-Bless the Lord, O my soul: and all that is within me. Bless his holy name. 2-Bless the Lord O my soul, and forget not all his benefits: 3-Who forgiveth all thine iniquities; who healeth all thy diseases. 4-Who redeemeth thy life from destruction; who crowneth thee with lovingkindness and tender mercies. 5-Who satisfieth thy mouth with good things; so that thy youth is renewed like the eagles."

Mae Mae could not take her eyes off of him. She rolled down the window of the limo to hear him clearly. Never before had she been so interested in the words of such a strange person. But his words seemed to salute her Baby better than any other words she'd heard this whole day.

'J Man' seemed not to notice that all attention was on him as he read and spoke to the crowd. He knew what he needed to say, and for whom and why it was intended. He needed no permission. He needed only to do what he was supposed to do.

"God has already forgiven our sins," he said. "Don't worry. Our Lord loves us so much that it's taken care of. Our loved one is with Him now. OK?"

He continued to read from his old ragged Bible. Psalm 103:11-For as heaven is high above the earth, so great is his mercy toward them that fear him. 12-As far as the east is from the west, so far hath he removed our transgressions from us. 13-Like as a father pitieth his children, so the Lord pitieth them that fear Him. 14-For he knoweth our frame: He remembereth that we are dust.'

"*God's child will be fine,*" he said, as he looked through the window at Mae Mae showing the most beautiful blue eyes and a wonderful smile. She'd never seen anyone like him before in her life. "*Your child will be just fine.*" He said.

It was a nice day with just a little mist in the air. The rains had come down hard all during the night, but now there was just a drizzle. Esther always hated the rain, but lately the things she'd hated so much in the past weren't all that bad.

She ran to the car trying not to get her hair wet. That could be a hassle. Wet hair was always bad news for most women. But at least she didn't have to worry about hers kinking up. She had what they called 'good hair' so it wasn't a big deal. But she still climbed in quickly and closed the door, momentarily getting away from the chilly wet day.

Traffic was somewhat light on Biltmore Avenue as she passed the donut shop and then the hospital. But she was deep in thought about all of the things going on in her life. She smiled as she thought about the fun time she and Jacob just had at the zoo.

As she pulled into traffic, as the signal turned to green, all she could hear was a loud bang. The car that came out of nowhere running through the traffic light, in the other direction had crashed into her driver's side.

Darkness captured her brain as she heard the faint sounds of the sirens rushing in her direction. Then there was nothing.

"Miss! Miss! Can you hear me?" An unfamiliar voice called out. "You just lay still. We've called your next of kin. OK?"

The lady was dressed in white from head to toe. Her smile was gentle and comforting as Esther looked at her through a haze. She walked back and forth, certain to keep a close watch on her patient. But Esther didn't know what hit her. She had no idea where she was or who was talking to her.

When Mae Mae arrived at Memorial Mission Hospital's emergency room. She had no idea which way to go. Sweat showed on her forehead and she entered and approached the information desk.

"'Scuse me, Miss, I'm lookin' fa my daughter, Esther," Mae Mae said, to the heavyset woman dressed in light blue scrubs, behind the window.

"Yes, are you her mother?" the nurse asked, with concern in her eyes.

"Yes Mam'! Yes Lord! She gone be alright?" Mae Mae asked. "I just got word an' rushed right ova here."

"OK, come with me," the nurse said, as she started walking. "We have her in a room back here. She was pretty shaken up. The officer said she got hit pretty hard right on her driver's side. I'd say she's pretty lucky to be alive. She has a broken arm and some internal bleeding. But she should be OK."

"Blessed be to the Lord!" Mae Mae shouted, entering the room behind the nurse.

"Baby! Baby! You a'right! It's Mama."

"She can hear you but she's under real heavy sedation"

"Mama," Esther said, in a weak, low voice. "Don't you worry, hear? Just make sure Jacob's OK. An' please Mama, call Frank."

The nurse allowed Mae Mae time with Esther to show her the love, support and reassurance needed to begin to take away the pain. But after a short while she escorted Mae Mae to the side to give her more details.

"As I was telling you before, Miss Redman, your daughter needs plenty of care and rest. She is basically going to be alright, but only time will mend her broken bones and internal injuries. I'll let the doctor tell you more when the x-rays come back. But she is going to have to stay here for a bit."

"OK," Mae Mae said, hearing from deep in a cloud, but not really hearing at all. "What kin I do? How kin I help? I just want her to be a'right," she said, bursting into tears.

"Well, the first thing you can do to help is to hold yourself together. Just remember it upsets her to see the folks she loves upset."

"OK! OK! I'll be strong fa her an' her baby boy."

Mae Mae sat at Esther's bedside all day. She made sure Little Jacob was taken care of and Jimmie was told so he could handle everything at the Café. Then as darkness approached outside the

window she decided to slip away to try to reach
Frank.

The pay phone was near the cafeteria. As
she walked, Mae Mae reached into her purse and
pulled out a dime and a handkerchief. She blew her
nose loudly, replaced it in her purse and then put the
dime in the slot. As she dialed the number she
thought about what she would say.

"Hello?" Mildred answered, wondering who
would be calling.

"Hello, this is Mae Mae Redman. I need to
git a hol' o' Frank. Is he at home?"

"No Mam' he ain't" Mildred said. "Can I
help you wit' somthin'?"

"Jus' have him call the Café soon as he can.
It's real important."

"Yes Mam,' I sho will."

Mildred hung up as her mind raced with
questions that no one was there to answer. "This is
gittin' real crazy," she said to herself. "One day his
woman callin' my house, then ha Mama got nerve
enough to call here. What in the worl' goin' on?"

It was getting late but before Mae Mae knew
it, she looked up from dozing in her chair and there
stood Frank. He stood silently, looking down at a
sleeping Esther with quiet tears flowing from his
eyes.

Mae Mae could see the love in his eyes. She
could see his wish that her pain would be his. She
had seen that same look in Jacob's eyes many,
many years ago.

"Shuh! He said, quietly. "I don't want to wake her. She seems to be resting. What in the world happened, Miss Mae?"

"Dey sayin' a car jus' pulled out on her. Car jus' ran da light an' hit her."

"Oh my God!" he said, making the sign of the cross.

"What's the doctor sayin'?"

"Well, dey sayin' she gone be fine. She got a broke arm and bleeding some inside. But thank da Lord, Frank! She gone be fine."

"Did she tell you about our drive to Cherokee?" he whispered.

"As far as I'm concerned Miss Mae, Esther found the Lord and was saved in that chapel on that mountain. Both of us felt the Spirit in that church that day, like you wouldn't believe. It was like the Lord knew how we've been waiting an' waiting so long for our love to be blessed. An' He finally answered our prayers."

"She tol' me, Frank. An' believe me, I knew love jus' like ya'll got. I tol' her dat too. I jus' want her to be happy, dat's all. She had a rough life before she left Asheville. In fact, my whole family done took too many generations to get it right. I was thinkin' maybe we finally did."

"Well I hope she told you just as soon as my divorce is final, I'm' not waistin' no time. I'm gone marry Esther so fast it's gonna make everybody's heads spin. I won't let her get away again."

They both set in the quietness of the room. Their thoughts of Esther had gone deep inside as they prayed for her recovery.

Esther slept through the night which the nurses claimed was a good thing. They all knew nothing but rest could help her at this point.

Frank kissed her lips as he departed, telling her that he would return later in the day. Mae Mae vowed that she would stay forever if needed. But she followed Frank out, and went toward the cafeteria.

When Mae Mae returned, the door to Esther's room was closed. Nurses were rushing anxiously in and out and all they said was for her to wait outside. When the doctor finally came out of the room, he had a look of despair on his face. He gently took her arm and pulled her to the side.

"Ma'm,' I must tell you that your daughter didn't make it. I am terribly sorry, Ma'm."

"What! Oh my God! What in the worl' happened? Dis mornin' she's just sleepin'. All ya'll kept sayin' she was gonna be fine." What da hell happened?"

"We don't know, Miss. The nurse said her vitals were great this morning. We have no idea what happened. I'm so sorry."

The nurse approached Mae Mae after the doctor left her. "I'm so sorry for your loss," she said. "I'm so glad that her sister was with her at the end. This lady came and demanded to see her. She said she was her sister, so we let her go in.

"She sat with her for a little while and then she left. After that, things just went downhill. I know it's very hard to lose a loved one. But it's easier when family is nearby."

"I don't know what you talkin' about," Mae Mae said. "Esther was my only living child."

EPILOGUE

'J Man' finished reading scripture and stood at the front door of the church. It was amazing that regardless of how large the church is, 'J Man' appeared larger than life.

None of them, including Mae Mae, knew where he came from. But somehow they didn't care. His words and his presence brought them to an unbelievable place of peace.

When he was finished, Mae Mae rolled the window up and leaned back in her seat. As the limo drove away, she looked over at Little Jacob and drifted into deep thought. Yes, she would raise him like her own. Yes, he would be the next generation. And yes, their family would not ever forget the past. They would continue to grow and learn from both the good and evil that made her the person she is.

Mae Mae loved Esther dearly. It seemed like one day Esther was giving her life to her God and Savior, and then she was dead. It was clear after their talk that Esther dreamed of having her baby and living 'happily ever after' with Frank and their babies for the rest of her life.

Tears flowed from Mae Mae's eyes as she looked again at Little Jacob and thought about the other grandchild that she would never see. "What in God's name happened?" she thought, sniffing and wiping her eyes. "They had no idea why or how my Baby died."

Mae Mae's mind had been in a cloud ever since Esther died. She could barely remember talking to Frank to make the funeral plans. They talked and planned just like they were family.

"He come talkin' 'bout he think Esther would want to have her 'home going' in the Catholic Church", she recalled. "An' I say, why, she wasn't no Catholic.

"I made up my mind exactly what to do when he say, 'When Esther was finally saved, it was in that little Catholic Church sitting on a hill in Cherokee. She fell in love with Jesus right then and there. She knew her sins were forgiven and she knew she was saved.'"

In their last conversation, Esther told Mae Mae how much she loved Frank and about definite plans for his divorce and their marriage. "They was so meant to be, dat even God knew it," she thought with a smile.

"Anyway, dat's why we at this Cath'lic Church way downtown today, for my Baby's funeral. It don't matter which church we ended up at. She fixin' to be wit' God"

The large black cars pulled away. And on both sides of Patton Ave, close to the church, crowds of people gathered and applauded. People from of all races and from all walks of life, were there to honor the star who sang, **"Strange Kind O' Love."**

www.ingramcontent.com/pod-product-compliance
Lightning Source LLC
Chambersburg PA
CBHW071946170626
46813CB00005B/1849